"I won't allow you to vanish from my life!"

"You won't have any choice."

"I make my own choices, Kristine. I've been waiting for you for a long time, and I'm not going to let you slip through my fingers. Two people can travel light—together."

"I don't believe that," she said with deep conviction.

"Then I'll have to prove you wrong."

Although born in England, **SANDRA FIELD** has lived most of her life in Canada; she says the silence and emptiness of the north speaks to her particularly. While she enjoys traveling, and passing on her sense of a new place, she often chooses to write about the city that is now her home. Sandra says, "I write out of any experience. I have learned that love with its joys and its pains is all-important. I hope this knowledge enriches my writing, and touches a chord in you, the reader."

Books by Sandra Field

HARLEQUIN PRESENTS
1336—LOVE AT FIRST SIGHT
1416—THE LAND OF MAYBE
1448—HAPPY ENDING
1506—SAFETY IN NUMBERS
1557—TAKEN BY STORM
1598—ONE-NIGHT STAND

HARLEQUIN ROMANCE
2457—THE STORMS OF SPRING
2480—SIGHT OF A STRANGER
2577—THE TIDES OF SUMMER

writing as Jan MacLean
2295—EARLY SUMMER
2348—WHITE FIRE
2537—ALL OUR TOMORROWS

writing as Jocelyn Haley
DREAM OF DARKNESS

SANDRA FIELD

Travelling Light

Harlequin Books

TORONTO • NEW YORK • LONDON
AMSTERDAM • PARIS • SYDNEY • HAMBURG
STOCKHOLM • ATHENS • TOKYO • MILAN
MADRID • WARSAW • BUDAPEST • AUCKLAND

ISBN 0-373-11646-2

TRAVELLING LIGHT

CHAPTER ONE

SHE felt at home.

It was ridiculous. Kristine was in Oslo, thousands of miles from home. She and her parents had left Norway when she was less than three, and she had grown up on a farm in central Canada; how could she possibly have concrete memories of this spacious, stately city? Yet, ridiculous though it was, she did indeed feel at home.

She had been strolling the length of Karl Johansgate, one of the main streets of Oslo, her eyes scanning the shop windows, the restaurants, the faces that passed her by. It was a fine evening in July and the sidewalks were crowded. As she wandered past an outdoor café, where experience had already taught her she could scarcely afford even a sandwich or a beer, she was oblivious of the male eyes that flickered over her, came back, and lingered, for she was immersed in her own thoughts.

This morning, at the border, she had almost turned back into Sweden, for somewhere deep within her she was afraid of this return to her birthplace, and of what she might learn here. Right now she was truly glad that she had taken her courage in her hands and driven past the checkpoint with its brave red, white and blue flag.

Farther up the street clowns were cavorting on the pavement, and a group of Bolivians in colorful costumes were singing folk melodies accompanied by drums and throaty flutes. Her mouth watering for a *pølse*, the Norwegian version of a hot dog, or for one of the baked potatoes the street vendors were selling, Kristine stopped to listen to the musicians. She had all the time in the world, she thought contentedly, aware that the long summer evening was gradually drawing to a close, the sky darkening above the buildings. The key to Harald's apartment was safely tucked away in one of the many pockets of her shorts, and he would not be back until the weekend. She was accountable to no one.

Another vendor tried to sell her a long-stemmed rose with petals the color of apricots. She shook her head, smiling, and said awkwardly, "*Nei takk.*" The language felt rough on her tongue. She should have made an effort to study it before she arrived. But then until last Saturday when she had phoned Harald she had not really been sure that she was going to come here...

A reggae singer attracted her attention, and then two young men in skintight black outfits with white-painted faces doing some very clever mime. The audience, she noticed, was mixed: tourists draped with cameras, indulgent middle-aged couples, and every now and then an archetypal Norwegian youth, tanned, blond, lithe and healthy. Her own hair was blond and her eyes blue. She fitted right in.

From the slim leather bag that looped over her shoulder and hung in front of her Kristine extracted enough money to buy an ice-cream cone, and because she was relaxed and happy her normal caution in a foreign country deserted her; she did not realize that eyes were following her for reasons other than her looks any more than she had noticed the girl watchers in the cafés. She heard music down one of the side streets and wandered in search of it, licking the mint-flavored ice cream.

The music came from a bar that she couldn't afford to enter. Then she saw a small leafy park farther down the street, and from beyond it heard the lilt of an accordion and the sound of singing. Even if she couldn't go into the bars and cafés it was fun to watch the people. A people to whom she was related by ties of birth, she mused, munching at the crusty cone as she followed the narrow pathway through the park in the direction of the singing.

In the last two years Kristine had travelled through Thailand, India, Turkey and Greece, and in none of these countries would she have walked alone at night through a city park, for she had a very healthy sense of survival and had soon learned to be streetwise. But this was Norway, and she felt at home, and now that she was finally here her mind was already dwelling on her next decision. She had a grandfather, father of her father, living in Fjaerland, a little village many miles north of Oslo. Her grandfather had no idea that she was here in Norway. Was she going to visit him?

She would have to decide soon, because her money was running out fast. Or else she would have to get a job to tide her over. Frowning to herself, some overhanging branches brushing her shoulder, she ducked into the shadows of the tree.

From nowhere a figure out of a nightmare sprang up in front of her. A grinning white face with a slash of red lips. Black-circled eyes. A black costume that was part of the shadows of the night. And hands that grabbed for her purse.

The hands were real. Male hands with dirty fingernails. Acting instinctively, Kristine thrust the remains of her ice-cream cone at his face, gathered her breath to scream and from behind felt another hand clamp over her mouth.

So there were two of them. Men dressed as clowns. How could she have been so stupid? So abysmally careless?

The man's fingers dug into her cheeks. His skin smelled acridly of greasepaint and nicotine, and it would have been all too easy for her to succumb to mindless panic. But Kristine had not been travelling for the better part of two years without learning a few tricks of her own. She sagged against her attacker as if overcome by fear, and reached for the tiny nail scissors that she always carried in her pocket. Twisting, she dug them into the first clown's hand, heard his yelp of pain, and kicked out viciously at the man behind her.

Philippe, with whom she had travelled in Turkey, had taught her that particular trick. Philippe had a face like a Raphael cherub and had been the meanest fighter she had ever seen.

The kick worked. And she was lucky. The second clown tripped over the iron bench on the edge of the path and crashed into the bushes. His curse, fortunately, was in Norwegian.

Adrenaline pumping through her veins, Kristine screamed as loudly as she could. The first clown swung at her with his fist. She ducked, hearing the swish of air past her ear, and struck out again with her lethal little scissors. As they grazed his flesh, his sideways swipe knocked them from her hand. But in the instant that he was off-balance she whirled and fled between the trees.

A branch struck her cheek as cruelly as a whiplash. Almost certain that the clowns were following her, she flung her body through the shrubs, burst out onto another path, and ran straight into the man who was waiting there.

Her gasp of terror drove the last of her breath out of her lungs. Yet even then Kristine did not give up. For Philippe had taught her something else. "Always you must have two weapons," he had said in his charmingly accented English. "One for every day, and one for the real emergency."

She had a Swiss army knife in her back pocket. Just before the man's arms could close around her, she hauled it out of her pocket in a blur of movement and raked the sharp point of the corkscrew down his bare arm.

He gave a grunt of pain. But he did not let go. Instead he pushed her away from him and said something urgent and incomprehensible in Norwegian.

He had been a fool to push her away, Kristine thought, and brought her knee up to his groin with malevolent speed.

His countermove was swift and decisive and her knee struck nothing but air. He gasped, "Stop! I'm trying to rescue you. *Je suis un ami... ein Freund.*"

Her fingers were already clawing for his eyes. Then her body went still as his words penetrated her haze of fear. For the first time she realized that he was not in a clown costume and that he was not fighting back: all his moves had been defensive. She said blankly, "*What* did you say?"

He was still clasping her strongly by the shoulders, the warmth of his fingers burning through her shirt. "I'm trying to rescue you," he repeated in English. "Against considerable odds, I might add. You did scream for help, didn't you?"

"Yes. Yes, I screamed... but I thought you were another one of them... the men who attacked me, I mean." She gave an uncontrollable shudder. It was very dark under the trees and she was still not quite sure she could trust him.

He added in a clipped voice, "Let's get out on the street where I can see you."

One hand slid to grasp hers, and he led the way down the path. Kristine's knees felt like jelly; she stumbled after him, and as the light from the street penetrated the trees, saw that her unknown rescuer was both tall and broad-shouldered, and moved with a fluid grace that seemed every bit as dangerous as the dead white faces of the clowns.

They came out on the pavement of a narrow street edged with rather grand stone buildings. The man stopped under the nearest streetlight, which was decorated with pretty baskets of flowers, and turned to face her, still holding her by the hand. In silence he looked down at her.

She was of average height. Her clothes—khaki shorts and a faded green shirt—were unremarkable, and her face was innocent of makeup. But the light shone full on her eyes, which were blue as gentians and still wide with remembered terror, and on a cap of short, feathered blond hair. Her features had the clarity of perfect bone structure, as such possessing an almost asexual beauty. Only in the tilt of her eyes and the sensual curve of her mouth was to be found her essential femaleness, a femaleness she was doing nothing to accentuate.

As for Kristine, she was instantly aware that her rescuer could have graced any advertisement for a Norwegian ski slope or a northern beach. Like her, he had blond hair and blue eyes. Yet the comparison ended there. His hair was darker than hers, tawny and streaked by the sun, while his eyes, gray blue like the sea on a misty day, were tumultuous with an emotion whose source she could not begin to guess. His nose was straight, his mouth well shaped, his jaw determined.

As the silence stretched out, she realized something else. Her survey of his external features could almost have been a defense mechanism. What she was striving to ignore was an intense and potentially devastating masculinity, focused at the moment entirely on her. To say he was attractive was to use that word only too literally.

She pulled her hand free. "I . . . thank you for coming to my rescue."

In disconcerting contrast to the stormy eyes, his face was expressionless. He said, "I think you were managing just fine without me."

He spoke English with almost no accent. "I—I thought they were coming after me," Kristine stammered, and realized dimly that she was still trembling.

"Who were they?"

"They were after my purse. They were dressed as clowns." She grimaced. "It was horrible, like a bad dream."

"I would gather you're a visitor here—don't you know enough not to wander around alone at night? Even though Oslo has a low crime rate compared to most European cities, pickpockets and drug addicts are everywhere."

Some of the turbulence in his eyes was anger, she realized belatedly, although it was an anger held in check and completely under his control. Yet because of his intervention he deserved an honest reply. "I'm not normally so careless," she confessed. "It was stupid of me."

"More than stupid. Criminally negligent...you're a very attractive young woman. It's entirely possible they wouldn't have stopped at theft."

Kristine lifted her chin. "Yet you yourself have just admitted that I got away from them on my own."

"So you are high-spirited," he said slowly. "Besides being very foolish."

"I'm not usually foolish!"

"Then why were you tonight?" he demanded.

"That's scarcely your business," she fumed, clenching her fists at her sides. As she did so, the cold metal of her Swiss army knife bit into her palm, and in sudden horror she remembered how she had dragged it down her rescuer's arm. She reached out and took him by the wrist, saying in consternation, "I must have hurt you— let me see your arm."

His shirtsleeves were rolled up. From his elbow halfway to the base of his thumb there was a long jagged gouge in his flesh, blood seeping from either side of it. She cried incoherently, "I'm so *sorry*, I didn't mean to hurt you, or at least I did because I thought you were one of them, and then of course you weren't..."

Her fingers were slender, and bare of rings. He said, a note in his voice she could not have placed, "Did you do the same to them?"

She looked up, sudden mischief lighting her face and driving away the last remnants of fear. "I was also carrying a pair of nail scissors," she said. "I used them to very good effect."

He gave a reluctant laugh, his gaze trained on her face. "Do you carry a first-aid kit, too? To minister to the trail of wounded in your wake?"

He was breathtaking when he laughed. Unconsciously Kristine's fingers tightened around his wrist. Under her thumb she felt the heat of his flesh, under her fingertips a supple shift of bone and tendon—intricate and indelible impressions as ruthless in their way as the anger in his steel blue eyes had been.

She let his arm fall to his side and heard herself say, "The apartment where I'm staying is only five minutes from here and I do keep a first-aid kit there. Will you let me wash that cut and put some antibiotic cream on it? It's the least I can do by way of reparation."

One by one her words repeated themselves in her head. You're crazy, Kristine, she thought. You should be running away from this man much faster than you ran from the clowns.

With a formal inclination of his head he said, "Thank you... My name, by the way, is Lars Bronstad."

"Kristine Kleiven."

"A Norwegian name, surely?"

"I was born here," she said crisply. "Shall we go?"

"Yet you speak no Norwegian?"

She did not want to tell anyone, let alone this handsome and disturbing stranger, the story of her upbringing. "I've lived in Canada ever since I was two," she said repressively. "Do you live in Oslo, Mr. Bronstad?"

"High-spirited, foolish, and a woman of secrets," he said, setting off down the street at her side.

"Everyone has secrets!"

There was an answering grimness in his tone. "True enough."

She did not ask what his secrets were. "So do you live in Oslo?" she persisted.

"On my grandmother's estate, north of the city. Asgard, it's called—my great-grandfather had more than his share of self-esteem."

Her brow wrinkled. "I'm afraid I don't understand."

"Asgard is the old name for the home of the gods."

She chuckled. "And they didn't call you Thor?"

"Thor was full of brute strength and not very bright—not exactly a compliment, Miss Kleiven."

"Kristine, please."

"And I am Lars. Are you staying long in Oslo?"

"I'm not sure what my plans are," she said evasively. "But while I'm here I have the use of my cousin Harald's apartment so I'm very lucky."

They talked about the high prices of accommodation and food until they came to the elegant stone building where Harald had a fourth-floor apartment. Kristine unlocked the security door and together they climbed the stairs. Now that she was here with Lars Bronstad, she was regretting her hasty invitation; Oslo seemed to be having a most peculiar effect on her, for it was not characteristic of her to invite a strange man to her room. Particularly a man as compelling as Lars. She hesitated outside the door, and said clumsily and untruthfully, "My cousin will be home later."

Lars said dryly, "You can leave the door open into the hallway if that will make you feel safer."

As she glanced back over her shoulder at him, the light fell strongly across the curve of her cheek. Anger hardening his voice, Lars demanded, "Did the men hit you?" Then with one finger he traced the reddening weal on her skin.

His lashes were darker than his hair, and his eyes had an intensity that disturbed her. "It's nothing—a tree branch when I was running away from them."

"I'll put some ice on it for you."

She turned away, unlocked the door and ushered him in, flipping on the light switch. Then she let the door close behind them; she already sensed that her safety where Lars Bronstad was concerned had nothing to do with an open door.

Although Kristine had yet to meet her cousin Harald, she knew quite a bit about him from the contrasts in his six rooms. Because the apartment with its high ceilings and oak floors was clearly expensive, and because he had several exquisite antiques, she was certain he had money. That he was untidy and did not believe in housework was self-evident. He also skied, played tennis, drank beer, and, judging by the delicious lace negligee hanging on the back of the bathroom door, had at least one girlfriend of equally extravagant tastes.

But Lars Bronstad quite effortlessly dominated Harald's large living room. He too looked expensive, she thought, noting his tailored summer trousers, well-fitting open-necked shirt, and crafted leather loafers. He did not look at all like Andreas, Bill or Philippe, young men with whom she had teamed up at various stages of her travels. It was not just that he was older, or that something in his bearing seemed to define the word masculine. There was something seasoned about him as well, as though his life had led him down some rough roads and the scars of travel were still visible. She said politely, "May I offer you a cold beer?"

He was examining the painting over the marble fireplace. "Thanks...your cousin has good taste."

In the kitchen she poured the beer into sterling-silver mugs. Then she fetched her first-aid kit from the guest bedroom and said, using his name for the first time, "Lars, if you'll come into the bathroom I'll wash your cut."

She was standing in the doorway. He said abruptly, "You look tired...did you just arrive in Norway today?" She nodded. "And you haven't been here since you were a little girl?"

"That's right."

"Am I way off the mark if I think it's not easy for you to be here?"

Every nerve in her body tensed. She didn't want Lars Bronstad guessing the confusion of emotion that had claimed her ever since she had headed in the direction of Oslo. "You can't possibly know that!"

His eyes narrowed. "I know it. I don't know how or why, but I do."

With a lack of finesse that secretly appalled her, Kristine snapped, "Look, I'm grateful you came to help me, and I'm truly sorry I hurt you—and that's that. My private life—my feelings—are nothing to do with you."

"We'll see."

Two small words into which he had injected a world of purpose. Her breath hissed between her teeth. An open door into the hallway was most certainly irrelevant as far as Lars Bronstad was concerned, she thought furiously. He was the most unsettling man she had ever met.

In the bathroom she turned on the taps in the basin. The room was graced with a sunken Jacuzzi, great piles of fleecy black towels, and rather more mirrors than were discreet; in one of them she watched Lars look around with interest. "A hedonist," he commented. "Why didn't he accompany his Canadian cousin on her first wanderings around Oslo?''

"He was busy," Kristine said with minimal truth, scrubbing her hands with soap and hot water, then guiding Lars's elbow under the cold tap. The flesh was swollen. Blood had encrusted his arm, so that the water ran pink into the bowl. His forearm was corded with muscle, and very tanned; blue veins stood out in the crook of his elbow. Her mouth suddenly dry, she turned off the tap and rummaged in her kit for the antibiotic ointment.

After dabbing his arm dry with a sterile pad, she daubed the cream on the long red gouge, her lower lip caught between her teeth as she tried to concentrate on her task. She had not felt the slightest bit like this when Philippe had been stung by a bee, or when Bill had scraped his knee on some rocks. Straightening, forcing herself to meet Lars's eyes, she said, "That looks better."

His face was very close to hers; she had no idea what he was thinking. His eyes were deep set, the sockets lined, and again she had the sense of a man who somewhere in his past had been stretched beyond his reasonable limits. Yet she had forfeited the right to ask him how or why, for she had discouraged him from a similar curiosity about herself. She bit her lip in frustration.

Lars reached around her with his other arm, turning on the cold tap again, and taking a facecloth from the nearest pile. "Hold still," he ordered.

As he brought the wet cloth up to her cheek, Kristine closed her eyes. He applied only the lightest of pressure, yet as she felt against her other cheek the waft of his breathing her heart began to race in her breast.

What was wrong with her? She'd never reacted like this to a man in her life; had never wanted to. Nor did she want to now. An unknown cousin and a problematic grandfather were males enough.

After what seemed like a very long time, Lars lowered the cloth and took her chin in his fingers. Kristine's eyes jerked open. She could lose herself in the depths of his eyes, she thought in utter confusion, and felt him angle her cheek to the mirror. "I suspect you'll have a quite dramatic bruise by tomorrow," he said.

For a wild moment she had thought he was going to kiss her. Hot color flooded both her cheeks. Lars said harshly, "I wanted to. Believe me, I wanted to."

Kristine's eyes flew back to meet his. Her vision had never been so keen, her sense of touch so acute; she felt herself being pulled into the blue of his eyes even as the warmth of his fingers on her skin spread through her body. All the normal barriers between two strangers fell to the ground, leaving the two of them, man and woman, sharing a moment of naked communication that shook her to the soul.

Then she jerked her chin free of his grip. The moment was gone, swallowed by the past, ephemeral as only memory could be. Kristine drew a long, jagged breath, knowing it was terror that had driven her to free herself, terror of a very different kind than that which had claimed her in the park. There was no room in her life for the stark honesty of that moment with its blend of sexual awareness and emotional intimacy, a blend that went far beyond the sexual into territory she had not even known existed. No room at all.

She grabbed a towel to wipe her face, avoiding his eyes. He said flatly, "Has that ever happened to you before?"

She shook her head; it was noticeable that she did not ask him the same question. He answered it anyway, and for the first time Kristine had a sense of English being a language foreign to his tongue. "Nor to me, ever. What does it mean?"

"Nothing! I'm tired, I had a bad fright, we're alone here—that's all."

Lars was breathing hard, and she was suddenly aware of the silent, empty rooms that surrounded them and of her distance from anyone she knew. He said, the words falling like stones, "I will not allow you to call it nothing."

In open defiance she said, "I'll call it what I choose."

"So you are a fighter, Kristine Kleiven." His smile was mirthless as his gaze dropped briefly to his gouged arm. "Not that I needed to be told that, did I? Perhaps we should go to the kitchen, where the cold beer is no doubt becoming warm beer?"

Although his change of subject threw her, her recovery was almost instant. "Flat, too," she said agreeably. "I made the mistake of pouring it."

"Your cousin isn't coming back tonight, is he?"

Her lashes flickered. "No," she said. "Not until the weekend."

"Yet you invite me—a stranger—up to his apartment. Do you go around looking for trouble?"

"I asked you here to make amends—not to be insulted!"

"You haven't answered my question."

She gave him a mocking smile. "You didn't have to accept the invitation, Lars."

"A fighter, indeed," Lars said, balancing lightly on the balls of his feet, and holding her gaze with his own. "I want to see you again. Tomorrow why don't we go to the Viking museum at Bygdoy?"

Normally there was nothing Kristine liked better than to tour a city with one of its inhabitants. "No, thank you," she said firmly.

"Every visitor to Oslo should go there."

"In that case I shall do so. On my own."

His jaw tightened infinitesimally. "How long are you staying in Oslo?"

"Not long."

"Then what's the harm in one outing?" he asked, his smile deliberately high voltage.

Fighting against his charm, she said, "I travel light."

"I'm not asking you to bring your cousin."

In spite of herself her lips quirked. "Earlier you called me foolish. I think it would be extremely foolish of me to accept your invitation."

"Merely high-spirited."

"You have an answer for everything and I need that beer," Kristine said feelingly, and marched into the kitchen. There she perched on a stool by the counter and launched a determined discussion of Ibsen's plays. Lars obligingly followed her lead. They moved to Grieg's music and drank one beer each. Then Lars stood up. Moving toward the door, he said, "What time will I pick you up tomorrow?"

"You're taking it for granted that I'm going with you!"

He leaned against the doorjamb, his body a long, lazy curve. His blue eyes were laughing at her again. "That would be very foolish of me," he said.

If she were sensible, she'd say no and oust this man from her life as violently as he had entered it. "I'll go," she said crossly. "Ten-thirty."

"Good." Lars pushed himself away from the door and crossed the hall to the main entrance. Pulling one of the tall double doors open, he said, "Lock this behind me, won't you? I hope you sleep well." Then the door shut and he was gone.

Kristine, who had been pondering what she would do were he to try and kiss her good-night, gaped at the gleaming wood panels, said a very rude word, and hoped she wouldn't behave as atypically during the rest of her stay in Norway as she had on the first day.

CHAPTER TWO

KRISTINE slept poorly. She got up early the next morning, washed out some clothes and hung them on Harald's balcony, and soaked in the Jacuzzi with a gloriously scented bubble bath that she suspected must belong to the owner of the negligee. She then dressed in her blue shorts with her favorite flowered shirt, breakfasted on the less dubious remains in the refrigerator, and went out to buy some groceries.

She had woken with Lars very much on her mind. But in the bright morning sunshine his effect on her last night began to seem the product of fright and an overactive imagination. He was only a man, after all. She would visit the Viking museum with him, there was no harm in that, and then they would go their separate ways. Jauntily she crossed the street to the market.

On her way back she dropped into the post office, finding to her delight that there was a letter in general delivery from Paul, her youngest and favorite brother, to whom she had mentioned the possibility that she might go to Oslo. Kristine sat down in the sun on a stone wall near Harald's street and tore the letter open.

Paul at eighteen was in love with basketball and women, in that order; he was putting himself through university on athletic scholarships and was now at a summer training session that happily was co-educational. After a two-page description of a center-forward called Lisa, he reported on the duty visit he had made to their parents recently. Mom was the same; Dad was suing the next-door neighbor for building a fence that infringed on his property.

Kristine let the closely written pages fall to her lap and stared blindly at the ground. She had done the right thing to leave the farm two years ago; as far as her family was concerned she had more than paid her dues. Yet not a letter came from home that she didn't feel guilty...

A shadow fell across the letter and a deep male voice said, "Bad news?"

Kristine gave a nervous start. Raising her eyes, she was presented with a close-up view of long muscular legs, navy shorts, and a shirt clinging to a flat belly. Lars. The gouge in his arm looked worse in daylight than it had last night. More guilt, she thought wildly, clutching at the thin sheets of airmail paper.

Lars sat down beside her on the wall, put an arm around her and said, "What's wrong, Kristine?"

His solicitude unnerved her almost as much as the warm weight of his arm. She shoved the pages of Paul's letter back into the envelope. "Nothing. Just a letter from one of my brothers... I haven't seen him for two years."

Lars glanced at the stamp. "You left Canada two years ago and you've been travelling ever since?" She nodded, her head bent. "Are you running from something—is that why you travel light?"

She was conscious of an irrational longing to pour out the whole sorry story to him. But that would be breaking a self-imposed rule she had never before been tempted to break. "I've already told you my private life is off-limits, Lars," she said more sharply than she had intended. She got to her feet, moving from the protection of his arm to stand alone. It was, she supposed, a symbolic action. Despite a father, a mother and four brothers, she had been standing alone most of her life.

And glad to do so, she thought fiercely. Stooping, she picked up the groceries. "Once I've put these away, we can go."

Lars leaned forward and neatly took one of the bags from her. Then he said in deliberate challenge, "Now you're really travelling light. Because you're letting me take some of the weight."

"That's not what I mean by it," she flashed. "I travel alone, Lars—*that's* what I mean."

"Not with me, you don't! When you're with me, we travel together."

The wind was playing with his hair. He looked as if he had slept as little as she, and on what was only their second meeting he was pushing his way inside boundaries that Philippe, Andreas and Bill had never once breached. "Then we won't travel at all," Kristine announced, her blue eyes openly unfriendly.

"Yes, we will. Because you know as well as I do how we met—we met because you screamed for help."

She glared at him, visited by the mad urge to scream for help again. "That's all very clever," she snorted, starting off down the street, "but you can't make me do anything I don't want to do!"

"I never thought otherwise," Lars said mildly.

She stamped her foot in exasperation. "For goodness' sake let's talk about something else. Tell me about the Vikings, since we're going to this museum. A good honest Viking with rape and pillage on his mind would be a lot easier to cope with than you, Lars Bronstad."

He stopped dead on the street and gave her a comprehensive survey from her overly bright eyes to her slim, tanned ankles. "You certainly bring out the Viking in me," he retorted, and watched as the flush in her cheeks deepened.

"Just don't even think of acting on it," she threatened.

"Not here. Not now."

"Not ever. Anywhere."

A transient gleam of humor in his eyes, he said, "I have a philosophic dislike for absolutes."

Disarmed in spite of herself, Kristine said sweetly, "You'd look really cute in one of those metal helmets with the horns on it."

"Historians have proved that Vikings didn't actually wear those helmets," he drawled.

"So is this museum going to give me a whole lot of boring facts instead of romance?" she riposted, and felt every nerve in her body spring to life at the answering laughter in his face. It was a good thing this was her last meeting with Lars, she thought. He was far more complex—and more dangerous—than any Viking could possibly be.

They arrived at the museum a couple of hours later, after a brief ferry trip and a leisurely stroll up the hill past houses with red-tiled roofs and gardens brilliant with roses and delphiniums. As they bought their tickets Lars said, "Just do your best to blank out all the other people," and then gestured to her to precede him.

The hall into which she walked had a high arched ceiling and long windows on either side. In the center of the hall was a ship made of dark wood, a ship whose hull was a graceful sweep from prow to stern. A tall mast stood amidships. High above Kristine's head the stem and stern ended in carved wooden spirals whose very uselessness emphasized their stark beauty.

She stood stock-still. Lars had told her nothing of what she might expect, allowing the full impact of the ancient vessel to strike her. She walked around it, then climbed the stairs and viewed it from above, with its oarholes and wide, slatted deck open to the elements; she wandered around the other two boats, the burial chamber, and the fierce wooden dragon heads. Finally, with a sigh of repletion she turned to the man who at no point had been far from her side and said quietly, "How brave they were, to set out across the sea not even knowing their destination...thirty men in an open ship."

"A ship shaped like a woman."

"And carved with images of death and war..." Her face bemused, she smiled at Lars. "Thank you...I wouldn't have missed this for anything."

As if he couldn't help himself, he ran one finger down the curve of her cheek. "I don't——" And then he stopped.

"What is it?" she asked in quick concern.

"Nothing...a silly fancy." He glanced down at his watch. "It's time to eat."

"You know something? You're a total mystery to me," Kristine said matter-of-factly.

He gave her a crooked smile. "I could say the same of you. Food, Kristine."

They found a restaurant by the water and ate smørbrød—open sandwiches with prawns and lettuce—and argued about aggression and the roots of war. Kristine was thoroughly enjoying herself, for Lars's intelligence was both wide ranging and tolerant. It was only his emotions that caused her trouble, she thought wryly. That and his sheer physical attraction: the ease of his long-limbed body in the chair, the gleam of blond hair on his arms, the latent strength in his hand as he poured more water into her glass. She insisted on paying her share of the bill, and then they passed between the closely packed tables on their way out.

Lars curled his fingers around her elbow. Like a stone thrown into water the contact rippled through Kristine's body. As they emerged on the street, he took her by the hand, another very ordinary gesture that filled her with a complicated mixture of pleasure and panic and reduced her to a tongue-tied silence.

They meandered along the streets until they came to a barrow selling cherries. Lars bought some, holding the bag out to Kristine. They were big ripe cherries like the ones her father used to grow before the orchard went into bankruptcy. She took one, biting into the dark red flesh, instantly transported back to the old farmhouse where as a child it had first become clear to her that something was badly wrong with her parents' marriage.

Juice was trickling down her chin. Lars said, "Hold still," and with a folded handkerchief swabbed her face. Then, taking her by surprise, he lowered his head and kissed her.

His lips were firm and tasted of cherries and flooded Kristine with bittersweet pain and an ache of longing. She pulled away, muttering frantically, "No, no—don't do that."

He said with a calmness belied by the rapid pulse at his throat, "I've been wanting to kiss you ever since last night." Then, as if nothing had happened, he offered her the bag of cherries again.

She fought to steady her breathing. How could she make a fuss when for him the kiss was already in the past? Anyway, she was twenty-three years old and both Philippe and Andreas had kissed her before she had made it clear to them that she was not interested in that kind of travelling companion. Determined not to let Lars know that the blood was racing through her veins from that brief touch of his mouth to hers, she helped herself to another cherry.

They took the ferry back to Oslo, past the crowded marina and the bulk of Arnhus Castle, and window-shopped near the city hall. In front of a display of hand-knit sweaters Lars said, "Where would you like to have dinner?"

"I can't afford to eat out twice in one day," Kristine answered lightly.

"I was inviting you to be my guest," he said with a careful lack of emphasis.

Almost glad that he had presented her with a genuine excuse, she said, "I can't do that, Lars. Because I don't have enough money to return the compliment."

"Your company is return enough."

Not sure whether he was serious or joking, she said, "You may think so, I don't."

"Kristine, you're a visitor in the city I call home. Let me at least introduce you to the delights of *sursild* and *rensdyr*."

"I'd be using you if I did that, don't you understand?"

He was clearly making an effort to hold on to his temper. "You have a conscience as scrupulous as a cardinal's!"

"I've met a lot of men in the last two years, and I've never wanted to be indebted to any of them."

"So I'm to be lumped together with everyone else?" he grated.

He was startlingly different from everyone else. Which she was not going to share with him. "It's a rule that's stood me in good stead," she said obstinately.

"Rules are made to be broken."

"Not this one."

Two American tourists in loud checked shirts were listening unashamedly to this interchange. Muttering a pithy Norwegian word under his breath, Lars took her by the arm and steered her out of earshot across the cobblestones. "Let's get something straight," he rasped. "Which is it—you don't want to have dinner with me or you can't afford to have dinner with me?"

Kristine let out her breath in a tiny sigh. It was a strange moment to remember the Viking vessel with its elegant curves and its aggressive crew, its unsettling combination of the feminine and the masculine. She said honestly, "I don't know, Lars. I do know I'm not looking for a summer romance——"

"Neither am I."

"Then what's the point? I'll be gone from here by Monday at the latest, and I won't be back."

"I asked if you wanted to have dinner with me. Wanted, Kristine."

She had never liked lying. "Yes, I want to! But——"

"Then tomorrow night have dinner with me and my grandmother at Asgard. That's free."

He had cleverly undercut all her arguments. "Right now you look as though you'd rather pick me up and shake me than have dinner with me," she remarked.

"Both," he said.

Surely there could be no harm in a family dinner. Besides, it might be her only chance to visit an old Norwegian estate. "All right," she said, "dinner tomorrow night."

Lars said with a touch of malice, "You should be more than a match for my grandmother. I'll pick you up at the apartment at six-thirty." He then wheeled and headed across the square.

Piqued that he should leave her so unceremoniously, angry with herself for minding, Kristine called after him, "You're just not used to being turned down."

He stopped in his tracks and looked back at her. "Kristine, if you're picturing me as some kind of Viking Don Juan wallowing through a sea of women, you couldn't be more wrong."

Even across twenty feet of cobblestone she could feel the pull of his body. "Are Norwegian women crazy? Or does winter freeze the blood in their veins?"

A smile was tugging at his mouth. "You flatter me."

Abandoning all caution, she said wickedly, "Clearly a female has to leave Norway at the age of two in order to develop a proper appreciation of a sexy man."

His legs straddled, the sun glinting in his hair, Lars said, "Certainly leaving Norway at the age of two has turned this particular female into a raving beauty."

Her jaw dropped. "Who, me?"

He looked around him. "No one else here."

"Raving beauties wear lots of makeup and elegant clothes and go to the hairdresser," Kristine argued. "I cut my own hair with my nail scissors—which, incidentally, I lost in the park last night."

He said evenly, "You are the most beautiful woman I have ever seen."

In the middle of a crowded public square was not an appropriate place for Kristine to be attacked by a sexual desire so strong that she was sure it must be obvious to every tourist within a hundred feet. Although she had never felt this way in her life, she could define exactly what she was feeling. She wanted Lars Bronstad, wanted him in the most basic way a woman could want a man. She said faintly, "I—I've got to go...I'll see you tomorrow," turned, and ran away from him across the square. Her face was burning, her eyes feverish...what must he think of her?

He thinks you're the most beautiful woman he's ever seen.

She should never have agreed to see him again tomorrow. Never.

Kristine spent the next morning in the National Gallery, where two Munch portraits caught her imagination. The first was of a young woman in a high-collared black dress, hands submissively folded, hair scraped back; the second was of a wild-haired, half-naked Madonna. Which one was she herself like? Or was she like neither?

Did travelling light mean that all her energies were confined to the cage of a narrow black dress?

She had no answers to her own questions. She only knew that the thought of seeing Lars tonight filled her with panic.

In the foyer of the museum she leafed through a phone book. There was no listing for a Lars Bronstad, no mention of Asgard, and she lacked the courage to tackle the operator with her minimal Norwegian. So she had to go to dinner tonight.

She set off down the street to the bookshop to buy a phrase book, trying to rationalize her dilemma. Lars was taking her mind off her grandfather. Once Harald returned—and providing the owner of the negligee did not object—she would spend some time with her cousin. And then she would be leaving Oslo. There was no need for her to panic.

Nevertheless, Kristine got back to the apartment in lots of time to get ready. Because she had only one dress, made of uncrushable jersey in a swirl of blues and lilacs, any indecision as to what to wear was eliminated. She shampooed her hair, soaked in more of the bubble bath, and made up her face with care. Her dress was designed for coolness, baring her shoulders and arms, hanging straight to her hips, then flaring out in graceful folds to her knees. Her shoes were thin-strapped blue sandals.

She looked at herself from all angles in the bathroom mirrors, remembering how she had gone dancing with Andreas in Greece and had flung the dress on without a second thought.

The doorbell rang. Her heart thumped against the wall of her chest and her wide blue eyes stared back at her as if they were not sure who she was any more. Taking a deep breath, Kristine went to open the door.

Lars was wearing a light gray summer suit with a shirt and tie; he looked handsome, formidable, and a total stranger. Her heart performed another uncomfortable maneuver in her breast. Ushering him into the foyer, she said weakly, "Hello."

In silence he looked her up and down. The dress touched her gently at breast and hip. Her neck looked long and slender, her eyes huge. He put the bouquet he was carrying on the cherrywood table and rested his hands on her bare shoulders, stroking her flesh with his thumbs. "The reason I do not often touch you," he said formally, his accent very much in evidence, "is because when I do I want only to make love to you."

The sensuous madonna and the black-clad woman rose in her mind. "I've never made love with anyone," Kristine said.

She saw his instant acceptance of her words. His hands stilled. "For whom have you been waiting?"

"I—I don't know...not for anyone. I——"

"You are so beautiful I forget the rest of the world exists," Lars said huskily.

If he kissed her now, she would be lost. Kristine stepped back, stammering, "Lars, I—I told you I travel light—I don't want involvement."

He let his hands travel the length of her bare arms. "Sooner or later you'll tell me why," he said.

The force of his will pushed against her defenses. "I don't owe you an explanation," she cried.

"I don't speak of owing or of debts—but of honesty," he said fiercely.

She took a deep breath. "Your grandmother can't possibly be as difficult to get along with as you."

His eyebrow quirked. "We shall see," he said. "By the way, these are roses from Asgard." He handed her a tissue-wrapped bouquet of old-fashioned blooms, heavy-petaled and fragrant, adding with his crooked smile, "They have thorns as sharp as your Swiss army knife—be careful."

"They're beautiful, thank you."

She arranged them in a lead-crystal vase, then she and Lars left the apartment. She was somehow not surprised that his car was a Jaguar, painted a sleek dark green. Within minutes they were in the countryside, winding up a low hill between tall, verdant trees. "My grandmother owns all this," Lars said. "The house is around the bend."

The house was a stone mansion that somehow repelled Kristine by the heaviness of its design and the blank stare of its long ranked windows. "Do you live here?" she asked noncommittally as Lars pulled up by the door.

"For now."

Which was a less than satisfactory answer, she thought, getting out of the car and walking up front steps guarded by a pair of hideous griffins. A uniformed butler greeted them and led them into the drawing room. Kristine had a quick impression of dark paneling, ornate furniture and gloomy oil paintings before Lars said, "Bestemor, I'd like you to meet Kristine Kleiven. Kristine, my grandmother, Marta Bronstad."

Marta Bronstad was seated in a high-backed wing chair, her crown of pure white hair held in place with diamond clips, her long gown of bottle green taffeta instantly making Kristine feel underdressed. With swift intuition she knew Lars would ordinarily have worn a tuxedo for dinner and had not done so tonight out of deference to her restricted wardrobe.

Marta Bronstad was holding out one hand, palm down; the smile on her lips did not reach her faded blue eyes. She expects me to kiss her hand, thought Kristine, and knew this was the first test. She said politely, "Good evening, Mrs. Bronstad, it's very kind of you to invite me to your home," took the proffered hand in hers and shook it.

"*Fru* Bronstad," the old woman corrected her.

"I speak almost no Norwegian, I'm afraid."

"Yet you were born here, Lars tells me. Why did your father leave his home?"

A question to which Kristine would very much have liked the answer. As the butler offered her a glass of sherry, she said, "Perhaps he wished, like the Vikings, to find a new and different land."

"And what did he do in that new and different land?"

Kristine's relationship with her father had never been easy, but she owed him more loyalty than she owed honesty to this inquisitive old lady. "He bought an orchard." She looked directly at Lars. "He grew cherries. *Kirsbaer*, you call them."

Between them the memory of a kiss flared to new life. Kristine looked back at his grandmother and asked, "Have you always lived here, Fru Bronstad?"

"Always. It will be the inheritance of my elder grandson, Lars."

So this dreary mansion would one day be Lars's. Somehow Kristine had not pictured him as a man content to wait around for his inheritance. She was almost relieved, because such a discovery lessened his attraction. Then Lars said levelly, "That is still to be decided, Bestemor."

Marta Bronstad glared at her grandson, transferred the glare to Kristine, and said, "Are you here to visit relatives, Miss Kleiven?"

For the first time Kristine's composure faltered. "Partly," she said. "I'm staying in my cousin's apartment, and I'll be meeting him on the weekend."

"Where did your father come from?"

"Fjaerland."

"Ah, yes...farmers," Fru Bronstad said dismissively.

Anger licked its way along Kristine's veins; she took a large gulp of sherry before she could say anything she

might regret. As Lars described the history of some of
the paintings in the room, Marta Bronstad sipped her
sherry in a silence that was the opposite to repose. The
butler made an announcement. In a rustle of skirts Lars's
grandmother stood up, took Lars by the arm and swept
out of the room. Kristine perforce followed.

The dining room table, large enough for twenty, had
been set at the far end with an intimidating array of
silverware and goblets. With a wrench of homesickness
like a physical pain, Kristine remembered the old pine
table in her mother's kitchen and the plain cutlery that
had come with them from Fjaerland. What was she doing
here in a house that she hated, with a woman who did
not like her and a man who liked her too much?

The meal began with thin strips of herring in a tangy
sauce. Kristine waited until Lars had picked up his cutlery
and chose the same knife and fork. Marta Bronstad said,
"Are your parents still living, Miss Kleiven?" Kristine
nodded. "And do you have brothers and sisters?"

Impatient with this catechism, aware that she was
speaking to Lars more than to his grandmother, Kristine
said, "I have four younger brothers, whom I virtually
raised—my mother hasn't been in good health for years.
When the youngest turned sixteen nearly two years ago
and left home, I too left. I've been travelling ever since."

"It takes money to travel," the old lady observed,
delicately dissecting one of the fillets.

"I've worked since I was sixteen, and saved every
penny I could. I also had temporary jobs in Greece and
France—and may have to do the same in Norway, pre-
suming I wish to continue to eat."

She smiled at the old lady after this smallest of jokes.
Marta Bronstad flicked a quick glance around the richly
appointed room and said frostily, "So you have no
money."

Lars made a sudden move on the other side of the table. But Kristine from the age of eleven had learned to confront her father, and was not about to back down to Marta Bronstad. Before Lars could intervene, she said with the clarity of extreme anger, "No, I have no money. Nor have I ambitions to acquire anyone else's money by fair means or foul."

"You're very forward, Miss Kleiven...young girls were not like that in my day."

"I saw a portrait in the National Gallery today of a young woman wearing a black dress that might just as well have been a straitjacket," Kristine replied vigorously. "I'm truly grateful I've been born in an age when I can travel on my own and earn my own money."

Marta Bronstad's eyes did not drop. "So you will continue your footloose ways when you leave here?"

"For as long as I have money and enjoy my travels, yes."

The old lady pounced with the speed of a ferret. "You don't consider you have a duty to your parents—to a mother who, you say, is far from well?"

Kristine flinched visibly; it was the chink in her armor, the guilt that grew with every letter from home. As the herring fillets wavered in her vision, she heard Lars rap out a sentence in Norwegian. Marta Bronstad's reply was unquestionably the Norwegian version of, "Humph!"

Kristine raised her head. Her eyes filled with an old pain, she looked straight at her interrogator and with desperate honesty said, "From the time I was six until I was twenty-one I raised my brothers, Fru Bronstad—what more must I do?"

"You always have a duty to your parents. Always."

The butler substituted a clear soup for the remains of the herring, and, having achieved her purpose, Marta Bronstad changed the subject. She spoke of the artist Munch, whom her mother had known, and of the sculptor Vigeland, whom she herself had known; she was caustic and entertaining and offered no apology for any of her earlier remarks. Although Kristine responded valiantly, the unaccustomed amounts of food and wine were giving her a headache.

The meal ended with some wickedly strong espresso served in tiny gilded cups in the drawing room. Then Lars stood up. "I'll drive Kristine home, Bestemor."

Kristine also got up. "Thank you for your hospitality, Fru Bronstad," she said, careful to keep any irony from her voice.

"As you're leaving Oslo soon, I doubt that I will see you again," Marta Bronstad said. "Good night, Miss Kleiven."

It was a dismissal. Kristine stalked down the steps between the griffins, got into Lars's car, and as soon as he closed his door said tempestuously, "What was that, Lars—some kind of test? If so, it's very obvious I failed."

"I would say you passed with flying colors."

"It was a setup!"

"My choice, you may remember, was to go to a restaurant."

This was not a statement calculated to appease Kristine's temper. "She thinks I'm after you for your money."

"Then she's wrong, isn't she?"

"I'm not after you at all!"

"She wants me to marry the girl next door, who's sweet and biddable and very rich. Sigrid is scared of my grandmother... she would never stand up to her as you did."

Almost choking with an inchoate mixture of jealousy and rage, Kristine sputtered, "Then marry Sigrid if you want any peace in the house. In the meantime, please take me home—I'm tired."

"In a minute," he said. Taking her incensed face in his hands, he bent his head and began kissing her. This time he showed no restraint, no holding back, his mouth burning through her defenses. Her lips parted on their own accord and as she felt the dart of his tongue like an arrow of fire all her anger and frustration coalesced into a passionate hunger. She looped her arms around his neck, dug her nails into his thick, springy hair, and kissed him back.

His response shuddered through his frame, as a tall tree shuddered in a storm. One of his hands caressed her back, bared by her dress; with the other he clasped her waist, pulling her closer. And still his mouth clung to hers, their tongues dancing, their breaths mingling.

Kristine's knee was doubled under her on the car seat; as pain shot through it, she made a small sound of protest, trying to straighten it in front of her. She was trembling very lightly all over, and wanted nothing more than to haul her dress over her head and make love to Lars in the back seat of the car.

He said unsteadily, "On at least one level you're after me."

What was the use of denying it? In a jerky, graceless movement she backed away from him, pulling her skirt over her legs. "I want to go home," she said, and had no idea whether she meant Oslo or Ontario.

Lars put the car in gear and surged down the driveway, gravel spitting from behind the tires. Trees flicked past, dark statues under a sky brilliant with stars. Kristine sat very still, hugging her chest, knowing that with one kiss she had crossed an invisible barrier and could never go back. Innocence had been lost. She now knew in her blood and her bones what it meant to crave the joining of a man's body to her own.

The lights of the city spangled the night like fallen stars. Lars drove down Harald's street, parked the car, and said with an urgency that in no way surprised her, "I want to make love to you, Kristine. Now. Tonight. I know we only met two days ago and that this isn't the way either of us normally behaves. But I have to know this is real—that you're real. That I can trust in—hell, I don't even know what I'm saying."

He raked his fingers through his hair. In the dimly lit car she gazed over at him, seeing the shadowed, deep-set eyes and the mouth that had seared its way into her soul. But on the drive from Asgard the turmoil in her blood had subsided a little, and her brain had started to work. She said quietly, "I can't, Lars—you must know I can't. We come from different worlds, you and I, and once I leave here we'll never see each other again—I'll never forget you but I won't make love with you."

"I won't allow you to vanish from my life!"

"You won't have any choice."

"I make my own choices, Kristine. I've been waiting for you for a long time, and I'm not going to let you slip through my fingers. Two people can travel light—together."

"I don't believe that," she said with deep conviction.

"Then I'll have to prove you wrong. What time can I meet you tomorrow?"

"We're not going to meet!"

"Yes, we are. I'll camp on the doorstep all night if that's what it takes."

He was entirely capable of doing so. Feeling besieged and frightened, Kristine repeated, "We're not going to meet and we're not going to make love—you must leave me alone, Lars."

Drumming his fingers on the wheel, he changed tactics. "My grandmother is a difficult and cantankerous old woman. But despite her money and her beloved Asgard she has had more than her share of tragedy...and I love her. She doesn't respect Sigrid—as I'm sure she respects you.''

"It doesn't matter what she thinks of me," Kristine cried. "Don't you understand that?"

"I'm refusing to," Lars said grimly. "I'm sure you've had more than enough of her right now—but, by one of those coincidences that I could do without, tomorrow is her birthday and I'm taking her out for dinner...I want you to join us."

Kristine didn't even hesitate. "No," she said. "Tomorrow's Friday and Harald will be back."

He bit off the words. "So Harald has more of a claim on you than I?"

"He's my first cousin and the first member of my family that I'm to meet...it's important to me," she said rebelliously.

Knuckles tight around the wheel, Lars said, "Then I'll phone you tomorrow morning."

She opened her door, said breathlessly, "I won't answer," and ran for the front steps of Harald's building. If she'd only stayed on Karl Johansgate the night before last, she thought sickly, none of this would have happened. And tomorrow morning would she really be capable of letting the phone ring unanswered?

The elevator creaked its way upward, slowly enough for her to decide that what she very much wanted to do was put her head on the pillow and have a good cry. Pulling out her key, she unlocked the door to the apartment.

A light was shining in Harald's bedroom.

CHAPTER THREE

STANDING in the hall, Kristine called uncertainly, "Hello...Harald?"

"Kristine—is that you? I got back early."

A young man swathed in one of the black bathroom towels came into the foyer. He had a shock of wet brown hair and a cheerful grin, and the hug he gave her was as brotherly as she could have wished. Kissing her on both cheeks Harald said, "This calls for champagne, this meeting of cousins after so many years. And how pretty a cousin you are," he finished gallantly.

No undercurrents in Harald, Kristine thought. She could travel anywhere with him and be quite safe. To her horror her eyes flooded with tears.

In quick concern he said, "You have a bruise on your cheek—has something happened?"

"It's a long story," she said shakily.

"I love stories and I love champagne. Let me put on some clothes and then you must tell me everything."

Under the influence of champagne on top of all the wine she had drunk Kristine told Harald a great deal, although not quite everything. He said decisively, "I'll take you out for dinner and dancing tomorrow night. You don't need another evening of grandmothers. You're sure you're not falling in love with the grandson, though? That would be very romantic."

Kristine sneezed as the bubbles of champagne tickled her nose. "Sex and romance aren't the same thing at all," she announced, just as if she knew what she was talking about.

"Combined they are irresistible, though," said Harald, raising his glass in a toast.

She and her cousin seemed to find quite a lot of things to toast as the night progressed. It was 3:00 a.m. when they went to bed, and at 9:30 Kristine woke up with a hangover. Probably the most expensive hangover she'd ever had, she decided, stepping into the shower and turning on the water full blast, a treatment that did not appear to help.

When she went into the kitchen, Harald took one look at her face and said briskly, "A light breakfast at an outdoor café, that will make you feel better."

It did not seem to be the time to assert her financial independence. "All right," she said meekly.

They walked out into the sunshine, which was blindingly bright. "Ouch," said Kristine, staggering a little.

Harald put his arm around her, dug into his shirt pocket and pulled out a pair of aviator's dark glasses, and positioned them on her nose. Then he steered her across the street. The man who had been seated on the stone wall watching all this got up and said tightly, "Good morning, Kristine."

The glasses made everything a surreal shade of blue and the man was Lars. Camped on her doorstep as he had threatened. Groping for her manners, Kristine said, "My cousin Harald...Lars Bronstad."

Lars gave Harald a curt nod, then reached out and removed the glasses. "What the devil have you been doing with yourself?"

"Champagne on top of wine," she said, blinking into the light and keeping a firm hold on Harald's arm. "What are *you* doing here?"

"I have to go to Lillehammer on business today. Spend the day with me tomorrow."

Harald said casually, "I'm going to the airport tomorrow morning, Kristine—my girlfriend's flying in from Milan."

She gave him a dirty look. Then she said ungraciously to Lars, "I suppose you can phone me in the morning. If you want to."

"Do you travel so light that you can't even commit yourself a day ahead of time?" he exploded.

"Don't yell, it hurts," she said fractiously. "I can't even decide which side of the street to walk on today, Lars."

Disregarding Harald as if he didn't exist, Lars seized her chin in one hand, kissed her full on the mouth, and then put the glasses back on her nose. "Tomorrow morning," he said, and strode away down the street.

Harald said, fascinated, "Well . . . you've made a big hit, little cousin."

"He's not used to women who say no. Harald, I'm in urgent need of coffee. Black coffee."

"He's in love with you."

"Don't talk nonsense—we haven't known each other for three days and all we do is fight."

"He's rich and handsome and crazy about you—are all Canadian women this fussy?"

"His grandmother wants him to marry the girl next door."

"Not a hope," said Harald. "That's a man who'll do what *he* wants . . . I think you should stay another week and give him a chance. Fjaerland will keep."

Kristine scowled at him. "Tell me about your work or your girlfriend or your new car, Harald. And please get me that cup of coffee."

Harald, after one look at her face, obliged on both counts. Kristine then went back to the apartment and slept through the afternoon. Harald's first comment

when she came out of the bedroom was, "Dress up—
we're going to the best restaurant in town."

Kristine felt a great deal better than she had this
morning. Giving him an impish grin, she said, "I have
one dress and you saw it last night."

"Maybe something of Gianetta's will fit you—come
along."

Half of Harald's closet was taken up by female
clothing. Utterly delectable female clothing. "I can't
wear something of hers, I haven't even met her," Kristine
protested, looking longingly at a slinky sea green
jumpsuit with spaghetti straps.

"She'd be delighted to lend you something," Harald
said. "She's very generous." Then he winked at her.

So when she and Harald walked arm in arm into an
elegant dining room that overlooked the royal palace
Kristine looked slim and sexy and every inch as though
she belonged there. As she was guided to her window
seat the first person she saw was Lars.

He was sitting at a circular corner table, staring at
her. He looked as though he had been struck on the head
by a blunt instrument.

The waiter put an immense, leather-bound menu in
front of her and asked her something in Norwegian.
Harald glanced over his shoulder to follow the direction
of her gaze, then looked back, an unholy amusement in
his face. "Of course, this is the obvious place to bring
his grandmother on her birthday—I should have thought
of that," he said blandly.

"Perhaps you did," Kristine snorted.

"I admit nothing. What will you have to drink,
cousin?"

"Anything but champagne," she said, and buried her
face in the menu. It had English subtitles. From behind
it she sneaked a glance at the circular table, met Lars's
eyes again, and ducked. He was with a party of five,

one of whom, seated beside him in a demure white lace dress, had to be the sweet and biddable Sigrid. It hadn't taken him long to find a substitute once she, Kristine, had turned down his invitation, she thought shrewishly.

Cocktails arrived; the menu was discussed with the solemnity due to a serious matter, then Harald put his linen napkin on the table and said, "Dance, Kristine?"

She had already noticed the rectangular parquet floor and the small dance band. Her brother Art had taught her how to dance; and it would beat sitting here trying not to stare at Lars. "Sure," she said.

The music was probably as lively as it got in these august surroundings; but Harald was a flashy and inventive dancer and Kristine was soon caught up in the rhythm of a jive. Her cheeks were pink and she was out of breath when he whirled her one last time and pulled her against his chest for the final chord. Then he said, taking her firmly by the hand, "It would be polite of you to wish an elderly lady the compliments of her birthday," and set off toward the circular table.

"Harald—don't!" she whispered fiercely, tugging at his hand.

"Are Canadian women cowards as well as fussy?" he whispered rhetorically, and kept going.

And Kristine, her breast still heaving from her exertions, thought recklessly, Why not?

Lars and a younger man, who was a less striking version of Lars, got to their feet. Harald greeted Lars, who then introduced his grandmother, his brother and sister-in-law, and Sigrid Christensen, who was even prettier close up than at a distance. A great many pleasantries were exchanged. Although Marta Bronstad looked less than delighted to see Kristine, Kristine wished her a happy birthday. From the fragments of cake left on the dessert plates, it was plain the party was almost over.

The band had struck up a waltz. Harald, with a charming smile, asked Sigrid to dance. Lars, without asking, walked around the table, took Kristine by the hand, and pulled her between the tables to the dance floor. Just before he took her into his arms, he said, "Bestemor invited Sigrid—I didn't." Then he put an arm around her waist, took her hand and pressed it to his chest, and began to dance.

His cheek was resting on her hair. The length of his body was hard against hers. Kristine made a tiny sound expressive of dismay, delight, and desire, and gave herself up to the slow rhythm of the music and the sensuality of an embrace unlike any she had ever known. Beneath her palm was the strong, steady beat of Lars's heart, an intimacy new to her. Against her hip she felt the instant and explicit hardness of his arousal; and that too was new and frightening and more exciting than she would have thought possible.

The dance seemed to last forever and was over before she was ready. There was a smatter of applause from the couples on the dance floor, and slowly Lars released her. He had, she knew, been holding her far closer than was correct, but she could not find it in her to chide him. His eyes brilliant with a mixture of lust and laughter, he said, "As you must be aware, I'm in no state to face my grandmother...perhaps you could walk in front of me?"

Kristine fluttered her lashes and said demurely, "So I'm to run interference? I'll do my best."

"We're in trouble enough with Bestemor without any outward manifestations."

She loved the twinkle in his eye and the sense of shared conspiracy. As her laugh rang out in a delicious cascade of sound, Lars added evenly, "When you look at me like that, you're no help at all."

For a moment his gaze dropped. Her backpack had not included a strapless bra; the jumpsuit therefore clung to her breasts, and the hot touch of his eyes hardened her nipples instantly. She said unsteadily, "Who's going to walk in front of whom?"

"Side by side?" he suggested.

Laughter bubbled in her throat again. "You're the one who has to live with your grandmother," she said, and set off through the tables ahead of him. His hand was resting lightly on the nape of her neck; she was sure her desire and her happiness—as deep as it was unreasoning—must be written on her face for all to see.

Harald was standing at the circular table chatting to Lars's brother, while Marta Bronstad was sitting rigidly in her chair, fury evident in every line of her body. Lars let his hand fall to his side, said to Kristine, "I'll see you tomorrow," then sat down. After a round of polite goodbyes, Harald took Kristine back to their table.

A tempting array of hors d'oeuvres on a silver tray had been placed on the starched linen cloth. Harald passed it to her and said, "The little Sigrid is charming and utterly unsuitable for Lars—it would be like mating a turtle dove with a falcon. She's also completely under the grandmother's thumb... I was delighted to see how indiscreetly you danced, cousin."

An elegant concoction of smoked salmon and capers fell from Kristine's fork and rolled onto her plate. Deciding subtlety would be wasted on her cousin, she said, "Harald, I'll talk about anything under the sun except Lars."

Harald replaced the tray on the table and said with unmistakable force, "I turned thirty last month, and I'm beginning to realize life doesn't give us as many second chances as we might think—be careful here, Kristine. This man Lars... unless my judgment's way off, I don't think he makes a habit of dancing like that. Nor, I would suspect, do you make a habit of responding as you did."

She stared at the intricately curled piece of fish. "I wish you wouldn't do this," she said in a low voice.

He gave a quick sigh of impatience. "Neither is it my habit to give advice to those I scarcely know," he said. "You should try this one—reindeer meat with cranberry relish." He then began to talk very entertainingly about how he had met Gianetta on a crowded railway platform in Vienna in the rain, and in the middle of this tale Lars and the rest of his party left. Little by little Kristine started to relax.

She was in bed by eleven, woke at eight, and joined Harald in cleaning up the apartment. At nine-thirty the phone rang. Harald passed her the receiver and she said with entirely false composure, "Hello, Lars."

He sounded distracted. "I'm back in Lillehammer—can I meet you around three?"

Unbidden, a picture of the young woman in the narrow black dress clicked into Kristine's brain. Against every lesson of the past sixteen years she said, "Harald recommended the Vigeland sculpture park . . . why don't we meet there?"

"By the monolith. Thanks, Kristine."

He hung up. "Congratulations!" Harald said.

"I must be certifiably insane," she answered succinctly. "Pass me that cloth."

While Harald vacuumed the living room, Kristine threw out most of the contents of the refrigerator and wiped the top of the stove. He cleaned the bathroom; she vacuumed the bedrooms. She then showered, changed into her blue shorts and flowered blouse and took the subway to the sculpture park.

Harald had loaned her a guidebook, so she knew as she went through the wrought-iron gates that the park contained dozens of sculptures by Gustav Vigeland.

However, the photos in the book had not prepared her for the reality.

She walked across the bridge with its monumental bronze figures, wandered through the rose garden, and listened to the splash of water from the great fountain upheld by six nude men. Human figures entwined with trees surrounded the fountain, figures from youth to old age, male and female, an inescapable cycle of endings and beginnings. Huge granite carvings stood in massive silence on the steps that led up to the monolith where she was to meet Lars. The monolith itself was more than she could bear, so full of energy and life force were its contorted forms.

She hurried back to the rose garden, knowing if she had any sense she would drive back to Sweden that very afternoon. Instead she listened to a young girl play Mozart on the violin by one of the parapets on the bridge, and put a coin she could ill afford in the open case on the ground. Near one of the ponds she ate the sandwich she had made at Harald's. Then she looked at her watch. Quarter to three. She'd better go.

Lars was not yet at the monolith. With deep reluctance Kristine stared up at it, a granite column fifty feet high carved with a writhing mass of naked human forms, life upon life, full of hunger, struggle, pain, and vitality. All the connections of one human being with another, she thought painfully. For not one of the figures was separate from the rest.

She felt tears prick her eyes. You can't travel light, she thought. It's not possible. I'm denying the human condition to do so.

There was a roaring in her ears and a block of ice seemed to have lodged itself in her midriff. Pulling her eyes away from the column, she saw Lars coming up the steps, his tall body superimposing itself on the seething bodies on the column. With all her willpower Kristine fought back her tears, wishing she were anywhere in the world but here.

Almost clumsily Lars took her in his arms. Surrendering to a pain she had scarcely known was hers, Kristine buried her face in his shirt and wept.

Her crying spell was short-lived but violent, her frame shaking, her arms wrapped tightly around his waist; and then she quietened. Lars pressed a couple of tissues into her hand, and dimly she became aware of other visitors tactfully skirting them, of a little girl staring up at her and asking a question of her mother. "I c-could scarcely have chosen a more public p-place in all of Oslo," she hiccuped.

"Let's find somewhere to sit down."

He kept an arm around her as they went down the steps. At the foot she was confronted by a granite sculpture of a man and a woman, leaning in toward each other and enclosing between them the child they had made. She said bleakly, "It was never like that in my family. I—I've never seen my father hug my mother. And *I* looked after the four boys—they didn't."

Lars said harshly, "No wonder you travel light."

They were crossing the mosaic floor by the fountain. "Are you angry with me?" Kristine whispered. "I know I must sound self-pitying."

"No, Kristine, I'm not angry with you. With your mother and your father, yes. With you, no."

She found a handkerchief in her pocket along with her Swiss army knife and blew her nose as they walked over the bridge. Lars led her down a slope into a small circle of statues that were encircled by bushes near a pond. "I didn't come here," she quavered.

"The children's corner, they call it."

He sat down on one of the benches while she went from one to the next of the bronze statues of babies and small children, memories of her brothers crowding her mind. When she finally sat down beside him, she leaned her head back on the bench and closed her eyes; she felt very tired.

"Tell me what it was like for you," Lars said.

Not looking at him she began to talk, and slowly there emerged the portraits of an angry father, of a mother who bore five children in as many years and coped by taking to her bed, and of a young girl, the only daughter, relegated to responsibilities beyond her years. "I didn't feel I had any choice," she said. "If I didn't look after the boys, no one would. Yet I loved them—of course I did."

"Loved them and resented them," Lars said. "Because they robbed you of your childhood."

"I suppose they did... I sure didn't have much time to play with the other kids. My brothers all left home as soon as they were old enough, and who could blame them? I stayed until Paul turned sixteen—he went to live with Carl in Manitoba—and then I left. My mother wept when I left," she finished in a dead voice.

"She expected you to stay although it was all right for the boys to leave?"

"That was the assumption."

"You had to get out in order to survive," he said sharply.

While he was telling her nothing she did not already know, to hear him say it was an immense relief. "Yes," she said.

The violinist was playing again. A sparrow flew over her head in a whirr of wings and at one end of the bridge a child was crying. Because she had wept in front of Lars, and because his embrace had comforted her, Kristine said with absolute honesty, "I decided years ago I never wanted to get married or have children, Lars. Love dies, and anger and depression take its place.

Children eat up your life and leave you nothing for yourself. So that's why I travel light.''

He was silent for a long time, his steel blue eyes resting on her face, which was still streaked with tears. Then he said, ''This whole park is about love and the lack of love, about the joys and costs of love. But it doesn't advocate closing yourself off from love—for that truly is death.''

The monolith had given her exactly the same message. She said stringently, ''I *know* how I feel about marriage and children—I grew up with a bad marriage and I raised four children.''

''Someone else's marriage and someone else's children.''

''That's all I've experienced,'' she said wildly. ''I don't know anything else!''

''Your own children will show you it can be different.''

His voice was implacable and his eyes bored into hers. ''I'm in no hurry to find out,'' she retorted.

''Let me come with you when you leave Oslo,'' Lars said softly. ''We'll travel together and I'll show you how a man and a woman can have fun and be happy.''

''I travelled with Bill in Thailand, and Andreas in Greece, and Philippe in Turkey and France—and we had fun.''

''And did you sleep with them?'' he rapped.

''I told you I didn't!''

''You and I would sleep together, Kristine—we would be together in all senses of the word. Day and night. Like a marriage.'' He ran one finger down the curve of her cheekbone to the corner of her mouth, tracing the fullness of her lower lip.

She said tautly, ''That's not fair, what you're doing.''

''It's called honesty. We want each other, why should we pretend otherwise?''

She dragged her eyes away from his. ''I won't travel with you, Lars. I won't.''

He said inflexibly, "Two years ago you did what needed to be done—you got out of your parents' house. Now the next step is in front of you. Take it, Kristine."

Honesty was the word he had used. "I'm afraid to," she said.

His lashes flickered. After a noticeable pause, he said, "Afraid?"

"Yes, afraid. Terrified, frightened, scared...you don't like me using those words, do you? But they're true."

"You may be afraid, and with good reason," he replied with painful exactitude. "But you're not a coward, Kristine. There's a big difference."

Her eyes fell on the long red line on his arm. Ten clowns would be easier to face than Lars, she thought, and remembered the blatant sensuality of the waltz they had shared last night. "You don't let up, do you?" she said shakily.

"No. Because I'm fighting for myself as well."

Unconsciously she moved away from him on the bench. "What do you mean?" she asked in a hostile voice.

There was another of those long moments of brooding silence before he spoke. "I don't normally pursue women who make it clear they don't want me around. Certainly I've never before wanted to tear the clothes off a woman on a dance floor. I don't like chasing you if you really don't want——"

"Then stop," she interrupted.

"I can't help myself."

Lines of tension were scoring his cheeks. Kristine hardened her heart. "I don't want marriage and I'm not into affairs," she said roundly, getting to her feet. "So there's no point in chasing me."

He too stood up. "Do you think I *like* feeling like this?" he said savagely.

"I can see that you don't," she answered, her nails digging into her palms. "I've been so confused since I met you that I've given you mixed messages and led you on, I know—I'm sorry about that. And I'm grateful you were so kind to me by the monolith. But there's nowhere for us to go, Lars. Let's end this now, before we begin anything we'll——''

"We began the minute you ran into me in the park."

"Then I'm sorry I ever did!"

"You don't mean that," he said.

She fought down the memories of his kisses and his laughter and the strength of his arms. "Yes, I do."

His body went very still. "Kristine, you're living out your parents' life—you're choosing fear over passion."

She clapped her hands to her ears. "I don't want to see you any more, and I have a perfect right to make that decision. Besides, I'm saving both of us grief further down the road."

"You're denying us any possibility of joy!"

"That's how *you* see it."

"You and me together—it feels so right."

"Stop it, Lars," Kristine begged. "I hate what you're doing to me."

All the expression drained from his face. "Hate's a strong word."

"You must leave me alone," she said in a quiet voice more convincing than any tirade. "I mean that, Lars. I'm not playing games or being hard to get—I just don't want to see you any more."

"We'll both regret this, Kristine."

"I know I'm doing the right thing," she said stubbornly.

His eyes were shuttered, like those of a stranger. "Then there's nothing more I can say, is there? Except goodbye...goodbye and good luck."

He gave her a brief nod, turned away and began walking up the path toward the bridge. As he disappeared among the crowds, Kristine sat down hard on the bench, gazing unseeingly at a bronze sculpture of a little boy.

She had not wanted Lars chasing her. And now he was not. Why then this empty hollow in the pit of her stomach, this sense of having murdered something new-born and vulnerable?

Kristine sat on the bench for the better part of an hour. She then walked back to Harald's place, the exercise making her feel minimally less unhappy. A long black car was parked near the entrance of the building, and as she approached a uniformed chauffeur got out. For a crazy moment she thought it must be a message from Lars, and her heart clenched.

The chauffeur looked old enough to be home with his great-grandchildren. He said in heavily accented English, "Fru Bronstad wishes to speak," and opened the back door of the car. The car looked just as old as he, but better preserved.

Kristine bent, saw Lars's grandmother sitting on the far side of the car, and got in with an unwillingness she did not try to mask. "Good afternoon," she said as pleasantly as she could.

Marta Bronstad inclined her head. Today she was wearing a linen suit with a lace-collared blouse, diamonds sending sharp-edged sparks from her ears and her fingers. She said coldly, "I won't take much of your time, Miss Kleiven. I want you to leave my grandson alone."

Wishing she could find this funny, Kristine said, "You could have saved yourself the trouble, Fru Bronstad. Because I've just finished giving him exactly the same message."

"I have difficulty believing that."

It had been a long day and Kristine was not in the mood for social niceties. "I really don't care whether you believe me or not."

Marta Bronstad sat up a little straighter. "Sigrid is a very suitable match for him, and a delightful girl. The marriage will join the two estates, and she will give him healthy sons."

The thought of Sigrid holding Lars's child lanced Kristine's body with pain. Aware at some level of the total irrationality of this response, she retorted peevishly, "Heaven forbid that she should give him daughters."

"I wish the Bronstad name perpetuated!"

Kristine drew a deep breath. "Fru Bronstad, you're wasting your time and mine. I'm leaving Oslo tomorrow, and I'm not coming back. I've already said goodbye to Lars."

Marta Bronstad's voice was fraught with suspicion. "When I die, he will be a rich man."

"There's obviously no point in me saying I don't give a damn about his money or his estate or his big stone house—I'd stifle in that house! Because you won't believe me, will you? But that's what I'm saying. And I'll say something else—Lars, unless I'm very much mistaken, will choose the woman he is to marry—the woman to bear his sons. Lars. Not you."

"Sigrid would never speak to me like this!"

Exasperated, Kristine rejoined, "Neither would I, if you'd stop interfering in my life and telling me what to do."

Marta Bronstad leaned forward, agitatedly twisting the diamond rings on her gnarled fingers. "I don't understand you, Miss Kleiven."

"You haven't tried to."

Some of the fire faded from the pale blue eyes that were glued to Kristine's face. "I suppose that's true," the old woman acknowledged with rigid fairness.

Kristine cast discretion to the winds, for what did it matter? After today Lars's grandmother, like Lars, would be gone from her life. "You saw me as a poverty-stricken tourist of dubious morals doing her best to snag your admittedly handsome grandson from under your nose," she said. "I may not have much money, but I don't operate that way. And the last thing I want to do is settle down on an estate in Norway. I don't want to settle down anywhere—with anyone."

The diamonds flashed their cold white fire. "I am beginning to think you are a most unusual young woman...and that I may have misjudged you."

A compliment, Kristine thought dazedly, and said with the utmost sobriety, "Thank you."

"Most unusual."

For the first time since they had met there was something approaching respect in the glance Marta Bronstad leveled at Kristine; and for the first time Kristine felt a twinge of liking for her adversary. She was not, Kristine would be willing to bet, a woman who often admitted she might have been wrong. "Well," she said inadequately, "I'd better be going." Searching for the word for goodbye, she held out her hand and said, "*Farvel*, Fru Bronstad."

Marta Bronstad shook her hand. "Goodbye, Miss Kleiven."

Kristine slid across the seat and the ancient chauffeur stood to attention as she got out. She ran for the door of Harald's building.

The last tie with Lars had been cut. And she knew precisely what she was going to do next. She was going to leave Oslo as soon as she could pack and load up her little car. Fond as she was of Harald, she did not want to be the third party to his weekend with the generous Gianetta. And the sooner she removed herself from the vicinity of Lars the better.

Practicing a determinedly bright smile as she ran upstairs, she girded herself to meet Harald's protestations and rang the doorbell.

CHAPTER FOUR

Two hours later Kristine was on her way. Harald had packed a substantial picnic for her supper, and Gianetta, a luscious black-eyed beauty, had insisted Kristine include the sea green jumpsuit in her backpack. "It takes no room and with your eyes—*bellissima*!"

Harald said bluntly, "What about Lars?"

"I've dealt with Lars," Kristine replied repressively.

"And are you going to Fjaerland?"

"I expect so. Eventually. But please don't tell them I'm coming, Harald."

He rolled his eyes to the ceiling in frustration, kissed her on both cheeks, and told her to phone any time in case of emergency. He then drew a map to guide her out of the city, and waved goodbye from the pavement as she drove away.

She took the E18 south. It was, she realized, the opposite direction to Fjaerland, but she needed time to absorb the loss of Lars before she faced her grandfather and all the family history that visit might involve. She drove steadily, her battered little Fiat eating up the miles; she wanted to put as much distance as she could between her and Oslo before she stopped for the night.

The countryside was very pretty, grain ripening in fields dotted with red barns, the farmhouses set among low hills. She camped past Larvik, by the sea, eating half her picnic for supper and then wandering along the shoreline, picking her way over the rocks. Although she was beyond Lars's reach now, she couldn't get him off her mind. Over and again her brain kept replaying every minute they had spent together.

She had a lot of memories of him, an astonishing number considering how brief a time they had known each other. But, she thought unhappily, she actually knew very little about him. She had had to get away from him to see that.

She watched a tern hover over the water and then plunge for a fish. Where had Lars learned such good English? What did he do for his living? Was he just hanging about Oslo waiting to inherit Asgard? She had asked him none of these questions. Because she hadn't wanted the answers? Or because she had wanted them too much?

He knew about her parents and her four brothers, and the way she felt about marriage. He must be thirty, yet he had not married. Why not?

Had he ever been in love?

She stooped and picked up a flat rock, skipping it across the surface of the water with absentminded expertise. Had her lack of curiosity hurt his feelings?

She would never know the answer to that question, or to any of the rest, she thought, gazing at the massed gray clouds low on the horizon. For she had chosen not to ask them. She had turned her back on any possibility of a relationship with Lars, a man as different from her four brothers as a man could be, because she was afraid of what might happen.

She walked back to the campsite and climbed into her sleeping bag, and the rhythm of the waves lulled her to sleep. In the morning the rest of Harald's picnic served as breakfast, eaten under a shelter because of the fine misty rain.

The rain worsened as she headed south again; she spent the afternoon in Kristiansand, then camped that night near Mandal. There was a beach at Mandal, and according to the tourist bureau it would be a sunny day tomorrow; perhaps a swim in the ocean would help ease the dull ache that seemed to be accompanying her wherever she went.

There was no reason for her to feel unhappy, she thought irritably, wrestling with the zip on her sleeping bag. Lars had done one thing, and one thing only: he had awakened her latent sexuality. That was all. She was a normal young woman and sooner or later somebody had to stir her hormones to action. Lars had succeeded where Bill, Andreas and Philippe had not. But that didn't mean she had to keep on thinking about him all the time. Or feel as if the weight of the world was sitting on her shoulders.

She punched her jacket and sweater into a pillow, put her head down and closed her eyes. There was a party going on somewhere up the hill, snatches of song and laughter drifting through the trees. As she burrowed deeper into her bag, into her traitorous mind flitted an image of Lars lying beside her, his hands on her body, his mouth, so well remembered, kissing hers.

Scowling into the darkness, cursing the two men in an Oslo park who had tried to steal her purse, she eventually fell asleep.

The next day was sunny and warm. Although Kristine had not slept well, the blue sky and gentle breeze raised her spirits. She breakfasted on fruit and sweet rolls, then walked the short distance to the town, whose main street had a series of little stalls bright with kites and balloons; the nearby beach was a long curve of clean, pale sand. Time for a swim, she thought, and headed back to the campsite to change.

Her tent was set apart from the rest under the trees. In front of it, sitting in a dispirited heap on the grass, was a very small boy. He was sobbing quietly to himself, his fist jammed in his mouth, his face streaked with dirt and tears. He had plainly been crying for some time.

Kristine walked across the grass and knelt beside him. "What's wrong?" she said softly.

He looked up at her with drowned blue eyes, babbled something in Norwegian, and started wailing in earnest. She brushed a mosquito from his ear, sat down on the grass, and took him in her arms. The language of comfort, she thought wryly, was universal. Rocking him gently, she sang him the lullaby that had never failed to work with Carl, who had had colic as a baby; as he quietened, she dried his tears with the tail of her shirt and played a finger game with him that had captivated all four of her brothers.

The little boy was no exception. He gave a gurgle of laughter and burbled another incomprehensible phrase. "I don't understand a word you're saying, love," Kristine announced. "But I would suspect you're lost. Shall we go and see if we can find your mother?"

He tugged at her fingers. "*Om igjen, om igjen,*" he said.

"*Om igjen?*" she repeated doubtfully.

A branch snapped in the trees. As Kristine looked up, a tall, broad-shouldered man stepped into the clearing, pushing aside a pine bough with one hand. "He wants you to do it again," he said.

Kristine's heart gave a great swoop in her breast and the little boy chanted, "*Om igjen!*"

Lars. Here at her campsite in Mandal, hundreds of kilometers from Oslo, his long body outlined by the green leaves of the trees, his blond hair lit by the sun. To give herself time to think, wondering how long he had been watching her, she played the game again. As the little boy butted his head in her breast, chortling with delight, she held him close and said with a calmness she was far from feeling, "Hello, Lars. What are you doing here?"

"Looking for you...is he lost?"

"You tell me," she said ruefully. "I can't understand a word he says."

The sun lancing through the trees dappled her body with a dancing pattern of light and shade; the child was now lying confidingly on her breast, his fingers clutching her shirt. Lars hunkered down beside them, addressing the boy very slowly, a smile softening his gray blue eyes. His face was only inches from Kristine's, so close that she caught the tang of his after-shave. He was wearing a loose-fitting shirt and cotton pants, and looked very sure of himself. The little boy muttered a reply, tears crowding on to his lashes again.

"His name is Leif and he can't find his mother," Lars reported briefly. "Did you just find him?"

"Just before you found me," she said, raising her chin in challenge.

His glance flicked over her and withdrew. "Let's check the campsites and the main gate," he said. "If that doesn't work, we'll try the town police."

He straightened, helping Kristine to her feet. For a moment his hands lingered on her elbow, his thumb smoothing her flesh. She had forgotten nothing, she thought helplessly; all the magic of his touch had been lying in ambush for her, waiting for his arrival. She jerked back, heard the child whimper in fright, and dropped her lips to his springy blond curls in compunction.

Lars said roughly, "This is one of the farthest sites from the gate—let's go up the hill." He set off ahead of her with long-legged strides.

The child was heavy. Kristine took her time, admiring the lean grace of Lars's movements and the way the breeze ruffled his hair, wishing she had the strength of character not to notice either one. He was stopping at each tent, many of which were deserted, asking the few people he found about the little boy. No one claimed him. But at the gate the attendant had been alerted about a missing child. "Two streets over and down a block," Lars reported. "The mother called half an hour ago."

"She must be so worried," Kristine said, shifting Leif's weight to her other arm. "Carl ran away once and it took me two hours to find him . . . the longest two hours of my life."

"Let me take him—he's heavy for you."

Heavy as her brothers had been heavy; and no one to help her with the burden. "I can manage," she said.

Lars leaned over and extracted the boy from her arms. "I know you can. No reason that you should, though."

Leif gave her a sleepy smile, said, "*Igjen*," and closed his eyes again. His lashes curved on his cheek in a way that entranced her—she who wanted nothing to do with small boys.

Unaware how vividly her features expressed her see-sawing emotions, she snapped, "Which way do we go?"

"Across the street."

His car was parked in the shade of a tree near the entrance to the campsite. They were halfway down the street the attendant had named when a little girl on a bicycle braked beside them, gave Lars a gap-toothed grin and a staccato message, and took off down the street. "His cousin," Lars explained. "She's gone to tell his mother."

Within minutes a woman in a pretty flowered dress was running toward them, her face distraught. When she saw the child in Lars's arms, she started laughing and crying at the same time. Lars passed Leif over. Leif woke up, saw his mother, put his pudgy arms around her neck in a stranglehold, and began bellowing at the top of his lungs. As the woman hugged him to her, pouring out her thanks, Lars explained it was Kristine who had found him, and in a flurry of gratitude and disclaimers they parted company.

Lars said, "Come on, I'll buy you an ice cream."

"I was going for a swim."

"We can do both."

"We?" she retorted snappishly.

"Or you and I—a foot apart on the sidewalk."

He was smiling at her in a way that melted her hostility as ice cream would melt in the sun. "You look different," she said.

"I feel different."

"Does your grandmother know you're here?"

"Indeed she does. After I discovered she'd been to see you, we had what Bestemor would call a difference of opinion and what I would call a fight. One of the things I told her was that I would never marry Sigrid."

"Is that why you look different?"

"I look different because I let you leave Oslo much too easily and I've enjoyed tracking you down. What kind of ice cream do you like?"

Kristine was not yet ready to capitulate. "How did you find me?"

"I have a good friend who just happens to be a police commissioner. Harald described your car to me, and the rest was easy—simply a matter of tracing it. Not many Fiats as old as yours still on the road."

"You wait until I see Harald!"

"He seemed quite pleased to hear from me," Lars said ingenuously.

"Huh!" said Kristine.

"Not as pleased as you are, though."

"Lars, nothing's changed."

"Yes, it has. I now know my own mind, for one thing."

"I've known mine all along," she retorted.

"Then I'll have to do my best to change it, won't I?" he said placidly. "There's the ice-cream booth—what would you like?"

"I want a triple cone with chocolate fudge, mint and butter pecan," she announced. "Then I'm going swimming."

"You'll sink."

"You let me worry about that."

"I'll have to come to your rescue. Again."

The glint in his eye was irresistible, and she was certainly pleased to see him. The sun was shining, Leif was restored to his mother, and she was going swimming in the North Sea with a man who was handsomer than any Viking. "I want peanuts on top of the ice-cream cone," she added.

"Whatever your heart desires."

"Not a statement I shall respond to," she said with a grandeur worthy of Marta Bronstad.

They wandered around the stalls, Kristine managing to get some of all three flavors of ice cream on her shirt, and then went back to the campsite so that she could change into her swimsuit. Then they walked to the beach, Kristine wearing a long T-shirt over her flowered bikini, Lars with his trunks under his clothes.

They crossed the pale, hot sand and put their towels down. Lars unbuttoned his shirt and let it fall to the sand, then stepped out of his pants. Kristine wrenched her eyes away and hauled her shirt over her head. She hoped the North Sea was cold. Her hormones were not just stirred up; they were running rampant.

Lars said casually, "It's quite acceptable to go topless on this beach."

She had already noticed that. "Not me," she said warmly.

Briefly his eyes rested on her small, firm breasts in their bikini top. "Too bad," he remarked with an exaggerated leer.

"Lars, what are you *doing* here?" Kristine said breathlessly, and knew the question was nonsensical as soon as it was out.

"Having fun."

"I'm glad one of us is."

He was openly laughing at her. "It would be nicer if both of us were."

"You can't do this to me!"

"I'm not doing anything to you—I'm not even touching you." He gave her body a comprehensive survey. "For which I deserve a medal."

"Very funny."

He suddenly dropped his bantering manner. "It wasn't funny at all on Saturday night when I realized I was never going to see you again. I drank too much aquavit and woke up on Sunday morning with a well-deserved hangover—that wasn't very funny either. I don't know what I'm doing here, Kristine—I only know that being with you feels right. And I'm damned if I'm allowing you to tell me otherwise."

After which inclusive speech he ran down the sloping sand, splashed into the sea and plunged headfirst into the waves. More slowly Kristine followed him. Dipping her toe in, she decided the North Sea was certainly cold. Lars had surfaced, his hair plastered to his skull, his eyes very blue against the water. "The temperature of the ocean and the Scandinavian lack of passion are in direct relation," he yelled.

Laughing, she ran to meet him, the water impeding her. She shrieked as a wave slapped at her waist. Then she too dived in, swimming underwater until his torso wavered in her vision. She burst up into the air and gasped, "Where did you learn to speak such good English?"

"London, New York and Brisbane."

Her eyes narrowed. But before she could ask anything else he said, "You don't tread water in the Norwegian Sea, Kristine—you swim. It's called survival."

She splashed him with the flat of her hand, he lunged toward her, and she slid sleekly under the sea again. She was a good swimmer because two of her brothers had been on the school swimming team and she had always loved the water. But she had never had as much fun in the pool as she had in the next fifteen minutes while she and Lars played a rough game of tag; nor was she at all sure that the water temperature could kill passion as he had claimed.

Of one accord they ran up the beach for their towels. Kristine dried her face and scrubbed at her arms, which were covered with goose bumps, and heard Lars say, "Has anyone told you yet today how beautiful you are?"

She glanced over at him. Water was trickling down his deep chest, droplets caught in his body hair. She swallowed. "Not yet."

"And you ask what I'm doing here?" He rubbed his shoulders with his towel, holding her gaze with his. "Somebody has to tell you these things, and I'd much prefer it to be me."

Her hands stilled. He had been taking in every detail of her body, from the slender length of her legs and the curve of her hips to the shadowed valley between her breasts; and for a moment all his passionate longing for her body was there for her to see, naked in his eyes.

Then he gave an exclamation of disgust and flung himself facedown on his towel on the sand, burying his face in the crook of his elbow. Kristine spread her towel next to his and sat down, finally able to observe him without herself being observed.

His legs were long and strongly muscled. His spine was a concave curve at his waist, rising to the taut buttocks under his brief swimming trunks. She said sharply, "What's that scar on your back?"

"Plane crash."

"Where?" she persisted.

"Malaysia."

She said with a careful lack of emphasis, "Just how long have you been living with your grandmother? And where were you before that?"

"Two months. Brazil. She had a minor stroke and I needed a break—so I came to help her sort out her affairs."

So Kristine's assumption that Lars had been waiting around for his inheritance couldn't have been more wrong. "How old are you, Lars?"

"Thirty-one."

Kristine had a host of other questions, but somehow the sunlit beach did not seem to be the place to ask them. Earlier she had told Lars she knew her own mind where he was concerned. The problem was nothing to do with her mind, she thought dryly; it was her body that kept betraying her. She reached in her bag for her suntan lotion, warmed some in her palm, and then, greatly daring, knelt at his side and began smoothing it over his back.

His shoulders tensed at her touch. His skin was damp and cool from the sea. She worked her fingertips into his muscles, sliding her hands down the arch of his ribs and up to his elbows; and all the while she knew she was playing with fire. When she finally stopped, putting the cap back on the lotion and sitting back on her heels, Lars twisted to face her, pulled her down beside him, and kissed her with a passionate hunger she more than matched.

Against her lips he murmured, "It's permissible to go topless on the beach...but making love is frowned upon."

Dizzy with longing, Kristine whispered, "Boring old Scandinavians."

His second kiss in its inventiveness and generosity was anything but boring. And her unabashedly sensual response taught her as much about herself as about Lars. "We've got to stop," she muttered. "We'll end up in the clink...which won't impress your friend the commissioner."

"Or my grandmother." As he eased his body away from hers, she kept her arms rigidly at her sides so that she wouldn't grab hold of him, and her gaze at the level of his breastbone so that she wouldn't have to meet his eyes. Lars said tersely, "Roll over and I'll put some lotion on you—you're so fair-skinned you could burn easily."

More playing with fire, she thought, and did as he asked. The slide of his hands down her rib cage was hypnotic, bathing her in heat, and she did not protest when he undid the strap of her bra, knowing he was learning the texture and lineaments of her body even as she had learned his. With every fiber of her being she ached to be joined to him, to experience all she was ignorant of; and for the first time in her life understood the power of her own sexuality.

Eventually he stopped, stretching out alongside her, one arm resting heavy across her back. Slowly the tumult in Kristine's body subsided; and as it did so she became aware of other concerns. Sand scratching her breast. The simple desire for a glass of water. And a cold, clear voice in her brain, a rational voice usurping the storm of emotion Lars had aroused.

You've never made love because you've always been afraid you'd get pregnant and end up like your mother, it said. But you would have made love with Lars on the beach and not given a thought to any of the consequences. You don't love him. You aren't going to marry him. How can you risk getting pregnant by him? Are you out of your mind?

That was exactly what she had been, she thought unhappily. Out of her mind and into her body in a way totally new to her. Nor was she at all sure, rational voice or no, if Lars were to kiss her in a place other than a public beach, that she could withstand him. She wanted him in a way that made nonsense of reason.

Even in the midst of her unhappiness she knew her options were limited. She could have an affair with Lars, for pregnancy could be prevented. Or she could get in her car and do her best to lose him again. And this time stay lost.

From the rhythm of his breathing she could tell that he had fallen asleep. She raised her head, noticing how his lashes lay on his cheek much as Leif's had, wondering what he had been doing in Brisbane and Brazil and Malaysia. It was a strong face, she thought, and a used face; whatever he had done had not left him unmarked.

The more time she spent with him, the harder it would be to walk away. Or, in her case, drive.

She fumbled for the straps of her bikini and did them up, and as she did so Lars's eyes opened. He said huskily, his face open to her in a way that weakened her very bones, "Ever since I met you, I've imagined waking up with you at my side."

What could she possibly say to that? Her eyes fell. She picked at the hem of her towel, knowing she had to get away, wondering how on earth she could outwit him. He said forcefully, "You're not ashamed of anything we've done together, are you, Kristine?"

"No," she said truthfully, "I'm not ashamed." Just terrified, she thought. My whole life, all twenty-three years of it, is telling me to run, when all I want to do is stay...

"Let's find some lunch."

They ate in a charming little restaurant overlooking the offshore islands, and then Lars said, "There's a hotel a couple of streets over—I'll book a room for tonight."

He was not specifying whether the room was for him or for both of them. But even as he had spoken a plan had dropped into her mind. Trying to look cool and sophisticated as though the hotel room was of no concern, simultaneously despising herself for the deception she was about to practice, Kristine said casually, "Lend me your keys and I'll drive your car to the hotel—I've never driven a Jaguar before."

He reached in his pocket and pulled out a key ring, showing her the ignition key. "The hotel's one street over from Leif's."

"Not far enough," she teased. "Maybe tomorrow I can drive it on the highway."

"Or we could go into Kristiansand tonight, go dancing."

She was never going to risk dancing with him again. "That would be fun...see you in a few minutes."

He was looking over the bill. She slipped between the tables, hurried out on the street, and once she was out of sight of the restaurant began to run. She ran all the way to her campsite, took her tent down in record time and stuffed it into her car, and then, with a fateful sense that she was altering her destiny forever, took Lars's keys and threw them as far as she could into the trees. Dimly she heard them clunk against a tree trunk, rustle through some branches and then fall to the ground.

She leaped into her car, drove to the gate, paid the attendant what she owed him, and turned onto the road. Taking a route that skirted both the hotel and the main street, she was on the main highway in a matter of minutes. Her plan was to drive straight to Stavanger. Stavanger looked large enough on the map that she could avoid Lars if by any chance he came after her.

But why would he? She was making it horribly clear that she wanted nothing more to do with him. And to top it off she had willfully deceived him and caused him considerable inconvenience. No, Lars would not come after her this time.

He would want nothing further to do with her.

CHAPTER FIVE

FOR the first few miles after she left Mandal Kristine was too agitated to pay much attention to the scenery; she found herself checking her rearview mirror constantly, as though Lars was suddenly going to appear on her tail.

He couldn't. She had thrown away the keys to his car.

He could send a police car after her, via his friend the commissioner.

And have to explain why an attractive young woman was fleeing him as fast as she could?

He wouldn't do that; it would be too embarrassing. She had seen the last of him. He would accept that she wanted nothing more to do with him, and he would go back to Asgard and to his grandmother.

But not to Sigrid. He had said he would never marry Sigrid.

With an impatient sigh Kristine shifted gears for a hill; the Fiat did not like sharp inclines. It was none of her business whom Lars married. In turning her back on all he represented, she had opted to travel light. So why was she even thinking about him? She was in Norway, the land of her birth; she could at least pay attention to the countryside.

By escaping from Lars in Mandal and heading for Stavanger, she had turned north. Fjaerland lay to the north.

She couldn't think about her grandfather either. Not when Lars was so fresh in her mind.

A rollicking mountain stream was following the course of the road; as she climbed higher it became a series of waterfalls, the foam white as snow. She rounded a curve and saw in front of her her first fjord, the sheen of light on the water hinting at the ice-cold depths below. She went through tunnels smelling of exhaust, she drove past the farms near Heskestad and the sheep country of Algard. And her rearview mirror remained empty of Lars in a police car with its lights flashing and its siren wailing.

Lars was not coming after her. In one act of deceit she had made sure of that.

She drove into Stavanger, got thoroughly lost, and more by luck than good judgment found the tourist information center near the harbor. The first thing she saw when she went in was a colored poster of an immense vertical cliff overhanging the impossibly blue waters of a fjord. "Where's that?" she said to the young woman behind the counter, any plans she might have had of continuing straight on to Bergen disappearing in a flash.

It was called Prekestolen, Pulpit Rock. It could be reached by ferry and car and a two-hour hike. She could catch the ferry the next morning. Which meant she needed a place to stay.

Armed with lists of youth hostels, campsites and guest houses, Kristine went outside. If by any chance Lars came after her, the first place he would look would be a campsite. She started phoning guest houses, and on her fifth try found one at a price considerably lower than the rest. She located it on the map, drove there, and parked outside.

It was in a very old building squeezed between two other buildings, and was clear proof of the adage that you got what you paid for. She went inside, inspected the room, which was a narrow cubicle containing a bed and a dresser, and paid her deposit. The landlady had wispy gray hair, spoke in a hushed voice, and had a nervous habit of continuously looking over her shoulder as though an unknown assailant was about to creep up on her. Kristine, who had spent a good part of the day worrying that Lars was going to creep up on her, brought in her backpack and left as soon as she could.

She spent the evening by the waterfront, feeding the gulls and watching the tourists, then eating grilled bacon, potatoes and tomatoes in a little café. Finally, reluctantly, she headed back to the guest house.

In the darkness its blank windows and stone stairwell were downright sinister. She had paid a considerable number of *kroner* for this, she wasn't going to back out now, Kristine thought stoutly, went inside, and unlocked her bedroom door. The house was utterly silent, as if she were the only occupant. It was a waiting silence, she thought with a little shiver, gathering up her toilet articles. She needed to wash the salt from her skin and her hair, salt that was a tangible and painful reminder of a man and woman frolicking in the waves and kissing each other on the pale sand...

She was thinking about Lars again, she realized, grimacing to herself and heading for the poky little bathroom. After an unsatisfactory shower with lukewarm water, she went to bed.

The ceiling needed replastering. The curtains did not fully close, letting in a cold white glare from the streetlights. There was not a sound anywhere in the house.

She had lied to Lars today, Kristine thought miserably; she had deliberately deceived him. The only time in her life that her father had ever struck her had been when at the age of five she had told him a barefaced lie. After that she had been too frightened to ever think of doing so again. Lars most certainly deserved better of her than that. Why hadn't she simply told him she didn't want to see him any more?

She had done that in Oslo. And it hadn't worked.

Her thoughts marched on. Was the real root of her fear that of getting pregnant? Or was that just a cover-up for a deeper fear, a fear that intimacy of any sort with a man would destroy the possibility of love rather than foster it? Five children to the contrary, there had been no love between her father and her mother.

The bed sagged and the pillow was rock-hard. Kristine forced her eyes shut. She counted sheep, then sea gulls and pigeons. She went to the bathroom, the plumbing gurgling through the pipes like an old man clearing his throat. She crawled back into bed and contemplated selling her car, taking the ferry to Bergen, and flying home. Home was known. Home was familiar. Home was a long way from Lars.

There was a clock near by that chimed every fifteen minutes. By two forty-five Kristine hated that clock. But the next time she heard it, it was ringing eight times, and the light falling into the room was the soft gray light of morning.

She would go to Bergen tomorrow, she thought, and in Bergen she would decide what she was going to do about her grandfather. Today she was going to climb Pulpit Rock. And she was going to pretend Lars did not exist.

Kristine left the guest house without a second look, knowing that if she spent another night in Stavanger it would be at a campground. At the market that was in full swing near the Vagen inlet where the ferries docked she bought fruit and pancakes for breakfast, eating on the stone steps and falling into conversation with a group of hostellers from Sweden. Afterward she went down to the dock and bought her ticket for the ferry to Tau.

Among the crowds milling around the fish sellers she suddenly saw a tall man with streaked blond hair, his back to her. Her heart did a flip-flop in her chest and for a moment she forgot to breathe.

The man disappeared into one of the pavement cafés. Had it been Lars? Although she had had only a fleeting glimpse of the back of his head, something in the way he held it, in the curl of blond hair on his nape, had reminded her forcibly of the man she was fleeing.

It couldn't have been Lars. Her pulses racing, she scurried away from the dock, up the stone steps and into the huge twelfth-century cathedral. The massive vestibule, the nave with its tall Gothic arches and the chancel crowned with glowing stained glass passed in front of her eyes like a dream. It wasn't Lars. She was imagining things. Imagining because deep within her she wanted to see him again?

Someone brushed her arm. She gave an exaggerated start. Whirling, her eyes wide, she saw a young man standing in front of her who bore no resemblance to Lars at all. Searching for words of apology, she gasped, "*Unnskyld meg.*"

"No sweat," he said in cheerful American slang, and turned back to his companion.

Kristine sank down on the nearest wooden chair. This was lunacy. She couldn't go conjuring Lars up at every turn; she'd go out of her mind. She took a couple of deep breaths, and gradually the ageless peace of the cathedral calmed her; by the time she had to leave for the ferry she had convinced herself that the man she had seen in the fish market was just another tall Norwegian with streaked blond hair. There were hundreds of them, after all. Slinging her small haversack on her back, she went to get her car.

She had been lucky enough to find a parking spot near the tourist bureau. She was unlocking her door when, without warning, a hand reached round her and wrested the keys from her grip. "Let me do that," Lars said unpleasantly, "since you're so good at losing keys."

She had not heard even a whisper of his footsteps on the pavement. He was holding her door open. Automatically she climbed in, stashing her haversack, which held juice, fruit and trail mix for her hike, on the back seat. Lars unlocked the passenger door, folded his long body into the seat beside her and said, keeping a firm hold on the key ring, "Where are you going?"

"I'm catching the ferry to Tau."

"I didn't think you'd be able to resist Pulpit Rock," he said, tossing the keys into her lap. "There's no point in taking two cars—let's go."

From the corner of her eye she saw that he was wearing bush trousers and well-worn hiking boots. "And what if I don't want to go with you?" she said.

"If you can climb quicker than I can, you can lose me on the way up," he said coldly. "I wouldn't hang around here. They don't take long loading the ferry."

Kristine put the key in the ignition and pulled out from the curb. Her instincts had been right: she had seen Lars near the market. Next time she'd do better to trust them.

She drove onto the ferry, parked on the lower deck, and locked the car again. In a silence that screamed with tension she preceded Lars up the metal steps to the upper deck. Within minutes the ferry pulled away from the stone parapet in a churn of foam. The deck was crowded with tourists, and cameras were already clicking as the ferry navigated the crowded inlet. Lars said with icy precision, "I don't feel like standing here making polite conversation with you and this is no place for the fight I'm spoiling for... I'll meet you by the car at Tau." Without a backward look he edged through the throng lining the gunwales and disappeared inside.

Kristine let out her pent-up breath in a long sigh. They steamed under a bridge and past some grain elevators, the air cool against her face. It would be a good day for a climb, she thought absently, not too hot.

The way Lars had sounded, he might just push her over the edge of Pulpit Rock. What had they told her at the tourist bureau? A vertical fall of two thousand feet.

She wandered up to the bow, the wind whipping color into her cheeks. Under a cloudy sky the sea was a dull gray, the low islands where sheep roamed slipping past one by one. Before she was ready for it, a loudspeaker announced their approach to Tau. She delayed as long as she could before trailing down to the lower deck, where Lars was waiting near the Fiat. For a moment across the rank of vehicles his eyes met hers, deep-set eyes livid with emotion. She winced away from them and got in the car.

Almost immediately the ferry bumped into the dock. "Turn right when you get off the boat," Lars said brusquely, then hid his face in the newspaper he was carrying.

Kristine was glad enough not to talk, partly because she had no idea what to say, partly because the narrow, winding road required her full attention and the signs for Prekestolen were inconspicuous.

When she eventually arrived at the hiking trail, she parked in the shade near the kiosk and pulled the keys from the ignition, tossing them in Lars's lap. "You don't have to climb with me," she said. "If you've got the keys and the car, I can't run away, can I?"

He shoved the keys in a buttoned pocket on his trousers and said flatly, "I need to climb a mountain or two—it's called sublimation. Are you ready?"

Too proud to beg him to stay behind, Kristine reached round for her haversack, very carefully avoiding touching him, and said with noticeable coolness, "Yes...would you lock the car, please?" Not waiting to see if he complied, she headed for the base of the trail, which was an unpretentious path through the trees.

Lars soon caught up with her. Aware of him treading soft-footed behind her through every nerve she possessed, knowing she couldn't put up with it for another five minutes, let alone two hours, she stepped sideways into the bushes and said ironically, "Why don't you go ahead? I wouldn't want to hold you up."

For a moment his eyes blazed at her with such primitive fury that she took a step backward, her feet crunching in the bracken. Then, as if someone had pulled a curtain across a window, there was only a pair of blank, steel blue eyes. "Fine," he said.

But he adjusted his pace so that he was always in her sight as they wound steadily upward through groves of jackpine, birch and mountain ash. Ferns rustled in the breeze. Far above them ravens swooped across the gray sky, their strident cries echoing among the cliffs.

They crossed a swamp on a boardwalk. Kristine sniffed the rich, peaty odor, trying to drag her eyes away from the lean, easy grace of Lars's stride; he looked as though he could keep it up for hours, she thought, batting at a mosquito circling her ear. And then they reached the base of a cliff and the climb steepened dramatically.

Halfway up she stopped to get an apple out of her haversack, knowing this was really only an excuse so that she could catch her breath, wishing she could share this small joke with her companion. She held out a second apple to him; he took it with a brief word of thanks, his strong white teeth biting into the flesh. She turned away, staring back the way they had come, where she could see the tiny figures of four people crossing the bog.

Lars tossed the core into the woods and started off again. Red-painted arrows marked the path across stretches of rock scraped bare by long-ago glaciers, while clumps of pink heather and yellow saxifrage overhung the dark water of mountain ponds. On the horizon rank upon rank of granite cliffs stretched as far as Kristine could see.

She would have been very happy were it not for Lars. His long legs were scaling the rocks as easily as if they were the steps of the cathedral, she thought petulantly, already feeling the pull at the backs of her knees and her thighs. Through his T-shirt she could see the ripple of his muscles as he pulled himself up a crevice; she found herself staring at his taut wrists as he gripped a rock for a lever, at the line of his thigh where the fabric of his bush trousers was pulled tight, at his thick hair disarrayed by the wind.

Because her attention was more on him than on what she was doing, her toes slipped on a patch of gravel and her knee bumped hard against a granite boulder. Although she bit off her cry of pain almost before it began, Lars turned instantly. Swiftly he reached down, took her hand, and drew her upright. "Are you all right?" he asked.

She could not bear the warmth of his palm on hers, the easy strength with which he had taken her weight. She snatched her hand back, rubbing it down the side of her jeans, and cried raggedly, "Don't *touch* me!"

His mouth thinned. "Do I repel you so much?" he snarled. "So much that you have to steal and lie to me?"

The heat of that brief touch was still searing Kristine's palm. She gave a wild laugh. "Is *that* what you think?"

"What else am I to think? You lie to me about my car, you take my keys so I can't follow you—why did you let me kiss you on the beach if that's the way you feel? Are you such a good actress that you can fake passion, melt in a man's arms when all the time you can't wait for him to leave you alone? To get out of your sight? Is *that* what you're like?"

He took a half step toward her. Flinching from the fury in his face, she stumbled against the same boulder, almost losing her balance. Again he reached out for her; but then, his fingers only inches from her arm, he stopped. His hand fell to his side. "I'm a fool!" he said with savage emphasis. "What in God's name am I doing, chasing a woman halfway across the country, a woman who hates me to touch her——?"

Kristine couldn't stand to see the self-contempt in his face. She said with frantic truth, "Try another version, Lars! Try that I liked your touch, your kisses so much that I was frightened out of my skin—so I lied to you and stole your keys and ran away from you. Try that one."

Abruptly she sat down on the boulder. Above their heads there was the scrape of boots and a tiny clatter of stones, and then a couple clambered down the rock face past them, smiling and nodding. "*God morgen . . . god morgen.*"

Lars answered them with automatic politeness. Kristine stayed silent; she had said more than enough, she thought, and waited for his reply with a hollow emptiness in her stomach. When the couple was out of sight, he said so quietly she had to strain to hear him, "Is that the truth, Kristine?"

"Yes, Lars, it's the truth." She took a deep breath. "I figured if I lied to you and lost your keys you'd be so angry you wouldn't come after me."

Her face was framed by ferns growing in a crack in the rock, and the wind played with the soft blond tendrils of her hair. Her eyes held his steadily. "I want to believe you," he said. "And that also is the truth."

"I'm sorry I lied." She bit her lip. "I didn't know what else to do."

The words torn from him, he said, "I wish you weren't so afraid of me."

"I can't help it!"

"It's like history repeating itself..."

So he had his own demons, his own ghosts from the past; and her actions had brought him face-to-face with them. "I've hurt you," she said miserably. "I'm sorry for that, too."

Wishing with all her heart that she could comfort him, she watched him rub the muscles in the back of his neck and give his shoulders a little shake. Then, as if he had made a decision, he took her hand in his, brought it to his lips, and pressed his mouth into her palm. He closed his eyes.

Near to tears, Kristine knew that for her this silent gesture bore an intimacy far greater than their passionate kisses on the beach. She opened her mouth to tell him so. But Lars had dropped her hand as suddenly as he had taken it. Glancing up at the sky, he said, "It's going to rain in the next couple of hours—we should hurry." Turning away from her, he began climbing as if a legion of mountain trolls was after him.

Kristine forced herself into motion again. The wind had freshened, so that the gray-edged clouds scudded across the sky. She tramped over scoured rocks and peat brown earth, trying to keep Lars in sight, and, not for the first time, wishing she could read his mind.

Rounding a corner, she found him waiting for her at the foot of a particularly steep part of the cliff. "I'll give you a hand here," he said.

She was glad enough of his help as she found toeholds in the rocks. He pulled her up the last few feet, and as she scrambled upright, brushing dirt from her jeans, she said wryly, "I keep remembering that we have to go back down."

"The view's worth it."

He took a step back from her. She said unevenly, "Lars, are you still angry with me?"

"No."

"I'm truly sorry I deceived you."

"It's past, Kristine. Gone." He gave her a faint smile. "We'd better keep going."

But was it gone? she wondered, noticing from the corner of her eye the first gleam of turquoise water far below. Had he really believed how afraid she was of the feelings he aroused in her? And what had he meant by history repeating itself?

The ground had leveled off and the walking was easier. Lars disappeared around a bend ahead of her. She followed him, then stopped dead in her tracks. In front of her, sharp-edged as a knife, loomed Prekestolen, the cliff called Pulpit Rock.

Its horizontal and vertical faces made an almost perfect right angle against the sky; its base was sunk deep into the blue-green waters of Lysefjord. In none of her travels had Kristine seen anything quite so spectacular.

There were two people walking across the flat expanse of rock, their bodies outlined against the clouds. She wanted to be there too, where granite and sky met. Lars said, grinning at the awestruck expression on her face, "Come on."

It was the first real smile he had given her since she had left him in the restaurant in Mandal. She smiled back. "You said the view was worth the climb. Understatement of the year, Lars."

"Didn't want you accusing me of nationalistic hype...how's your head for heights?"

"Fine, I guess. I had no trouble hiking in Greece."

He stepped back so that she could precede him. Leaning against the wind, she walked across the last of the trail and stepped onto the huge square top of Prekestolen.

The sinuous curve of Lysefjord, cupped by rounded gray cliffs, vanished mysteriously into the clouds and the mist. But Prekestolen ended sharply, like the ax blade of an ancient Viking, a clarion call to violence and to death.

Unable to help herself, Kristine walked across the seamed, split rock, bracing herself against the relentless push of the wind. Dropping to her knees, and then lying flat, she crawled up to that quivering juncture of solidity and space, of matter and nothingness, and looked over the edge.

Like an ambush the water swooped up to meet her; the rough rock beneath her chest and thighs vanished. In pure horror she felt herself being pulled nearer the edge, her fingers losing their hold, her body weightless as a leaf in the wind. The cliffs flung themselves toward her. The sky swirled in front of her like a whirlpool, drawing her inexorably into its embrace.

As though from another planet she felt hands clasp her hips and haul her backward, strong hands tight around her body. Her fingertips scraped across the jagged granite; from deep within her throat she was whimpering with fear. She closed her eyes, but still the sky whirled and spun and she was falling, falling, falling...

Lars's voice, deep and resonant, said, "Kristine, relax your fingers—it's okay, you're safe, I've got you."

Her cheekbone bumped on an outcrop of rock, the pain so sudden and unexpected that she was shocked into some kind of awareness. Her eyes flew open. All she could see was rock, veined and craggy like the face of an old man. Rock. Not sky.

Lars let go of her hips. Kneeling at her side, he slid his arms around her waist and pulled her up against his chest, her body so limp that she seemed boneless. Then he stood up, and from a long way away she heard an unknown voice ask a concerned question and Lars make a reassuring reply. He walked back from the edge as far as he could go, until they were under the overhang of the cliff, sheltered from the wind and from the curious gazes of the other hikers. Then he stooped again, holding her in his lap, chafing her cold hands in his warmer ones.

She was trembling lightly all over. Just as she trembled when Lars kissed her, Kristine thought numbly, and thrust her face into his chest.

He held her close, repeatedly smoothing her shoulders, murmuring to her in Norwegian. She had no need to translate; they were the words of comfort, as far from anger and disillusion as they could be. Clutching at his shirt, wanting nothing but the truth between him and her, she said incoherently, "Lars, I've never made love with anyone because I've always been afraid of physical intimacy... over the years I could see my father and my mother draw further and further apart. With each child that was born they seemed to hate each other more, so by the time I was twelve I was telling myself that I was never going to get pregnant and I was certainly never going to get married—why should I? It was like a cage, a trap. No joy, no laughter...only a man who was angry all the time and a woman who used illness to hide herself from life."

She rubbed her sore cheek against his collarbone. "And children meant work—always something to do for them, always watching them and worrying that something would happen to them and I'd be blamed because I was the one who was supposed to be looking after them. When all I wanted to do was play with my school friends and have fun...was that so very wrong of me?"

"It wasn't wrong at all."

"And then you came along." She glanced up at him, seeing the tiny black flecks in the smoke blue of his irises. "What you showed me was that I'd managed just fine for twenty-three years because I'd never met a man who made me feel like a woman. A—a sexual woman. I'd never known how the touch of a hand, a kiss—even a look—could make nonsense of all my fears and misgivings, could drive me so strongly toward you so that I forgot caution and only wanted you, the man..."

She drew a long, shuddering breath. "But as soon as I was away from you I was terrified of what was happening to me. Scared out of my wits that I'd end up like my parents, trapped and resentful and loveless. So, in Oslo and again in Mandal, I ran away. I didn't know what else to do."

She had run out of things to say. Feeling drained yet oddly peaceful, because she knew every word she had spoken had been the truth, she rested her face on his chest.

Lars was silent for a long time, so long that she felt a return of the dizzying terror that had seized her on the edge of the cliff. She had misjudged him, she thought. He didn't want her honesty. Perhaps all he wanted was to bed her. So her incoherent confession of fears and resentments that went back to childhood was far more than he had bargained for.

He said finally, "I didn't understand how deep it went. Even after you cried at the monolith I didn't understand."

"Perhaps all you want is a summer affair," she blurted.

"I've never said that."

What do you want? The words were on the tip of Kristine's tongue. But how could she ask them, when she had no idea what she herself wanted?

Lars eased her body away from his. "Are you feeling better now?" he asked.

Knowing nothing had been settled, yet too tired to push for resolution, she said, "If that's what vertigo feels like, no wonder I stay away from Alfred Hitchcock movies."

Lars's smile stopped short of his eyes. He helped her to her feet. "Why don't you look around for a while? But stay away from the edge."

She took his advice, letting the grandeur of the view sink into her senses, wondering if she was being fanciful to imagine that Lars had within him both the uncompromising hardness of the rock face and the mysterious depths of the fjord so far below. She did know something. In that moment of swirling horror at the edge of the cliff she had made two decisions. She was going to see her grandfather. And, if Lars still wanted to, she would like him to travel with her.

She had been afraid of intimacy for too long.

Four hours later Lars was driving the Fiat off the ferry in Stavanger. He parked to one side, letting the other cars pass, and said evenly, "I'm booked into a hotel just up the street. I'd like to take you to dinner."

"All right," Kristine said.

Something flashed across his face and was gone. With a lightness that did not quite ring true, he said, "What, no arguments about money?"

"Not tonight, Lars. Tomorrow," she said pertly.

"In that case, we shall have caviar and champagne...where are you staying?"

She gave a witty, more or less accurate description of the guest house, and finished, "So I guess I'll stay at a campsite."

"As your financial scruples are on holiday, I'll book you a room in my hotel."

Every muscle in her body ached. "Will it have a bathtub? With hot water?"

"It's a very good hotel, I don't think you have to worry."

She would wear the sea green jumpsuit that Gianetta had given her, Kristine thought, and remembered how she and Lars had danced together in another restaurant in Oslo. "All right," she said again.

The hotel was indeed elegant, yet Lars in his dirt-streaked bush trousers and hiking boots looked entirely at home there. Her backpack and haversack were ceremonially loaded on the porter's trolley, her car was parked for her, and she was given a room on the same floor as Lars's but four doors down. Lars followed her into it and tipped the porter, who then left, closing the door behind him.

Kristine's eyes had flown to the queen-size bed with its very beautiful tapestry bedspread. Lars said forcibly, "Let's get something straight, Kristine. Now, before we go any further. I'm not going to let you disappear again——"

"I don't want to disappear," she said.

Triumph, happiness and a fugitive relief lit up his face. "Good," he said laconically, his smile turning her knees to water. "But I want to take a break from all the demands I've made on you. Physical demands. So let's just have fun together, do all the tourist things—hike a bit, swim, enjoy ourselves. I don't know whether you're going to see your grandfather or not, but even if you don't you should go to places like Geiranger and Dalsnibba... and I want to be with you when you do."

She said, feeling as though she was picking her way among the rocks on Prekestolen, "You don't want to make love with me any more?"

"That's not what I said. I want to, but I'm not going to—because I can see the conflict that causes you." He leaned over and kissed the tip of her nose. "I'd appreciate it if you wouldn't wear that turquoise outfit, though—there are limits to my self-control."

There was something wrong here. Wrinkling her brow, giving him a dubious smile, Kristine said, "What if *I* change my mind? If I want to go to bed with you?"

His body was still; but his eyes, raking her from head to toe, betrayed him. He said huskily, "I want you to decide that when we're nowhere near each other. Not even in the same room. Do you understand what I mean?"

"To decide with my head and not my hormones," she said lightly, and knew as soon as the words were out what she should have said. She should have said, To decide with my head and not my heart. And what did *that* mean?

Lars moved around her to the door, and for the first time it occurred to Kristine that he was as wary of the bed as she was. "I'll pick you up for dinner in an hour?" he asked.

"That's fine," she said, and watched the door close for the second time. Other than a kiss that one of her brothers could have given her, Lars had not touched her at all. Nor would he, she thought. The next move was up to her.

She scowled hideously at the bed, bounced up and down on the mattress a few times, and resolutely squashed any fantasies of her and Lars sharing that bed. Because essentially he was right. They each knew he could sweep her off her feet, that he could seduce her with one kiss. They also each knew how nervous she was of any commitment to physical intimacy, let alone emotional closeness. Oh, yes, he was right.

Which did nothing for the fierce hunger that gnawed at her when she pictured Lars stretched out beside her on the tapestry bedspread.

She unzipped her backpack, shook out her blue dress and left the jumpsuit rolled up in a ball underneath her socks. Then she turned on the bath taps, cheering up somewhat when she saw the array of complimentary soaps and shampoos—a distinct improvement on last night. And, when all was said and done, Lars wanted to travel with her. Wanted it enough to pursue her from Mandal.

She'd better tell him tonight what she'd done with his keys.

CHAPTER SIX

HAVING laid her monetary scruples to rest for one evening, Kristine thoroughly enjoyed her dinner with Lars. The food was delicious, and the wine made her feel wittier than usual and more penetrating in her judgments, as well as—and here she was brought up short—more desirable as a woman. Luckily there was no dance floor.

After they had eaten, they strolled down to the harbor, going into a couple of bars and joining a group of singers in the second one, Kristine warbling away happily at Lars's side. The bar was crowded; he therefore kept very close to her, his shoulder against hers, his arm going around her once or twice to prevent her from being buffeted by the rowdier elements in the bar. She liked this very much, so much so that to distract herself she tried to pick out all the languages she could hear around her. Over the last two years she had decided she wanted to study languages when she went home, and perhaps become an interpreter. In the meantime she must work on her Norwegian with Lars. If—when—she went to Fjaerland, she didn't want to be totally dependent on a dictionary.

Lars had just ordered a second beer when a red-haired man of about his age started pushing his way through the throng toward them and came to a stop in front of her companion. He said, grinning from ear to ear, "You're Lars Bronstad, aren't you? Remember me? Kevin Armstrong, Canadian team, slalom." He stuck out his hand.

Lars took it, although not before Kristine sensed through the sudden rigidity of the arm pressed against hers his reluctance to do so. Then Kevin transferred his grin to her, shaking her hand and repeating his name. She liked him right away. After introducing herself, she discovered he had once lived only thirty miles from her, in Welland. "Did you say you were on the Canadian ski team?" she asked.

"Yeah...got beaten by this guy more than once." And he gave Lars a friendly punch on the arm, the beer sloshing in the mug in his other hand.

Lars said, in a not very subtle shift of topic, "So what are you doing here, Kevin?"

"Filming beer commercials for a company back home. Fjords and pretty girls in national costume, you know the sort of thing. Pays well, that's for sure. What are you up to these days?"

"Living in Oslo for the moment, looking after some family business."

Kevin raised his mug. "You can't afford to drink beer in Oslo. Mind you, I'm doing okay...turned pro three years ago. It's too bad you retired, Lars. You could have gone places." His face sobered. "I was sorry to hear about your wife. I suppose that's why you quit, eh? Must have been a bad time for you."

"Yes," said Lars. "Well, it's been good seeing you again, Kevin—I hope you enjoy the rest of your stay. Kristine and I are planning an early start in the morning, so we'd better head back to the hotel."

His hand closed around Kristine's arm in a grip that brooked no arguments. She, the word "wife" still reverberating in her brain, said with a composure that amazed her, "Nice meeting you, Kevin. Good luck with the commercials."

Lars steered her through the crowds, and for once the touch of his hand on her flesh did not arouse her to lust.

As they emerged on the pavement, Lars dropped her arm, his face set in grim lines that discouraged any conversation, and began hurrying up the hill toward the hotel. Kristine's blue sandals were not designed for speed, and she had already climbed Prekestolen that day. She said, "Kevin's not chasing us, Lars."

Lars slowed his pace. "Sorry."

"I'm sure he realized you didn't like him mentioning your wife...he didn't strike me as insensitive."

He looked down at her, his eyes like flint. "I don't want to talk about it."

"I didn't even know you'd been married," she cried, adding in a rush, "I'm assuming that you no longer are."

"She died eight years ago. I said I didn't want to talk about her!"

Out of a pain that made nonsense of discretion, Kristine said, "You still love her."

"I don't! For God's sake drop the subject, Kristine."

If he was angry, she was equally so. "Are there any other little surprises that I'm liable to trip over if we travel together? If so, I'd like to be warned right now."

"I would have told you about her sooner or later."

"Forgive me if I doubt that." As quickly as her temper had flared, it died down. She said gently, "Won't you at least tell me what happened to her?"

"Some time, maybe. But not tonight."

"You're behaving like a stereotypical male—you know that, don't you? All stiff upper lip and let's not talk about feelings."

He said tightly, "I'm choosing not to discuss what was the worst year of my life late at night on a crowded sidewalk with a woman I scarcely know—that's what I'm doing."

A woman I scarcely know...

Left with nothing to say, Kristine set off at as fast a clip as her sandals would carry her, heartily glad that she and Lars had separate rooms because at this precise moment she couldn't wait to get rid of him. She stalked through the lobby of the hotel, stood in an ostentatious silence as the elevator carried them to their floor, and said with minimal politeness as she passed his door, "Good night."

"I'll meet you for breakfast at eight."

Maybe, she thought. And closed the door to her room with exaggerated quietness.

Despite a conviction that her seething emotions would keep her awake all night, Kristine slept fairly well. Her rage had disappeared in the night, her hurt not entirely. She did wake to the certainty that Lars, like her, had elements in his past that had scarred him; he was treating her scars with respect and she should do the same. So when she knocked on his door at five to eight, showered and wearing her jeans with a man-tailored pale yellow shirt, the first thing she said to him was, "I shouldn't have lost my temper last night."

His mouth twisted. "I didn't behave particularly well either—I could have done without Kevin being the one to tell you I'd been married."

He too was wearing jeans, his wet hair curling around his ears, a damp towel looped over his bare shoulder. Kristine added hastily, "I'm early—I'll come back later."

"It's okay, I won't be a minute." Lars stood aside so that she could enter, scrubbing at his hair so that it stood up on his head in little spikes; as he did so, the muscles played across his belly. Kristine gulped, turned away, and heard him mutter, "We don't even have to touch each other, do we?"

Striving for the tone of voice with which she had controlled four small boys, Kristine said, "I think you should put your shirt on."

However, he started brushing his hair in the mirror first. "I suppose a good-morning kiss would be against the rules that I was foolish enough to set up."

"Definitely," she said.

"You don't sound as decisive as you should." Walking over to her, Lars bent his head and teased her lips apart with his. He then proceeded to kiss her with thoroughness, expertise and undoubted pleasure. When he let go of her, he reached for his shirt, and only a close observer would have noticed that he had trouble with the buttons because his hands were not quite steady.

Pink-cheeked and flustered, Kristine said indignantly, "That's not fair!"

"Come on, Kris, you know as well as I do that life's not fair."

"All my brothers call me Kris."

"I don't think you're in any danger of confusing me with them," he replied.

Kristine didn't think so either. She said at random, "What are we going to do today?"

"I think we should take the ferry to Bergen. It would be better to take my car as it's more comfortable. We could leave yours in a parking lot where you pay by the week."

"I've thought about that," she said candidly. "Even though it puts the cost up for me I think we should take both cars as far as Fjaerland. I have no idea what kind of reception I'll get because I have no idea why my father left there—I only know he would never talk about it. So my grandfather might not let me over the threshold—or he might invite me to stay for a month. If he does invite me to stay, you might want to go back to Oslo."

"That makes sense," Lars said slowly. "Although I don't like the thought of you driving the mountain roads in that little car of yours—it must be almost as old as you are."

"It was all I could afford . . . and it hasn't let me down yet. Anyway, you'll be right in front of me."

"Okay. I'll make the ferry reservations and we'll plan to stay a couple of days in Bergen."

Deciding she might as well deal with any arguments before breakfast, Kristine added, "I don't want you to think that I'm ungrateful for this lovely hotel, Lars. But I'm not going to make a habit of letting you pay for me—it'll be campsites for me from now on."

"In that case," he said, raising one brow, "I'll buy myself a tent this morning before we leave. Otherwise travelling together won't be anything but an academic exercise."

"One that would keep us out of mischief," she said limpidly.

"But you might get bored," he responded with a gleam in his eye.

"Around you? Not likely."

"Breakfast, Kristine," he said with mock sternness. "And, as it's included on the hotel bill, I'm paying."

She dropped him the best curtsy she could in her jeans, which fit her rather snugly, and then ran for the door before he could grab her. They were both laughing as they walked to the elevator.

Somehow this beginning to the day set the tone for the next three days, days they spent in Bergen, city of seven mountains. They ate lunch in a tavern in Bryggen, where the town was founded in the eleventh century, and that afternoon they took the funicular, a steep little railway, to the peak of one of the mountains. They went to the stave church in Fantoft, built out of wood over eight hundred years ago; it creaked in the wind as Kristine imagined the Viking ships must have creaked on the waves. That evening they went to a concert at Troldhaugen, Grieg's home, and saw his tiny red studio nestled among the trees by the lakeside. On their last day in Bergen Lars bought Kristine a huge bunch of sweet peas in the market; without telling him, she pressed two of them between the pages of her passport, wanting a concrete memento of three of the happiest days of her life.

Although she and Lars, far from making love with each other, were behaving most circumspectly, the crackle of sexual tension bound them together, often unacknowledged, always powerful. She had learned a lot about him during their stay in Bergen: his formidable control over his sexuality; his sensitivity to music; his ability to play the fool; his care of her. From the story of her childhood and adolescence he had somehow divined that the girl growing up in a family of seven had nevertheless suffered terribly from loneliness, and was making sure that with him she never had to feel lonely.

Such companionship was new to Kristine. She basked in it, feeling herself open like a flower to the sun.

They left Bergen in the rain, which did not damp her spirits in the slightest. She sang to herself as she followed the dark green Jaguar through tunnel after tunnel, past waterfalls and forested hills and cherry orchards. At Kvanndal they took a ferry across the wide sweep of Hardangerfjord, where Kristine fell into conversation with some American tourists. They had just come back from Ulvik and gave the little town on the shores of the fjord a glowing recommendation. When Lars came up on the deck to join her, she asked, "Are we planning to go to Ulvik?"

His face changed. "No," he said. "It's not on our way...we're only taking this ferry so you can see the orchards in Lofthus."

"I was just talking to some people who've been there— they said it was very pretty. Right on the fjord, and so peaceful."

"You're going to see more than your fill of fjords, Kris."

His unexpected opposition perversely increased her desire to go to Ulvik. "They were telling me how warm the water is for swimming, because it's at the end of the fjord. We're not in any hurry, Lars—let's go there."

"I'd rather not."

She recognized that face; he had looked the same after talking to Kevin in the bar in Bergen. She gave him a long, thoughtful look. "Maybe I'll go on my own, then. We can meet up somewhere else later on—in Voss or Gudvangen."

In a small gesture whose violence shocked her, Lars banged his palm hard on the rail. "You must do as you choose," he said.

Kristine had no idea why her simple request had roused such strong feelings in him, and was quite sure it was useless to ask. She wandered off, watching the approach of the village of Utne, its little white houses clustered against the hillside.

Their stop there was brief. They disembarked at the next stop, then drove south to Lofthus, through orchards laden with ripe red fruit. Lars pulled up by the side of the road, and he and Kristine walked along a track in the grass between the cherry trees. The track widened, and in front of her she saw through the gentle drizzle the looming mountains on the other shore and the white sprawl of a glacier among the peaks.

Lars said flatly, "I'll go to Ulvik with you."

Baffled, she stared at him. They were utterly alone, the wet grass brushing her bare legs, swallows swooping through the sky over their heads. "Won't you tell me what's wrong?"

"My wife's buried there. I haven't been back for years."

The words had been wrenched from him. Then that formidable control, a control she had seen before, clamped down on his features. She said, knowing her words for the truth, "I'm not the only one who travels alone."

"You see too much, Kristine."

She was not at all sure he meant the words as a compliment. It was on the tip of her tongue to say she had changed her mind, that she no longer wanted to go to Ulvik, supposedly so peaceful, in actuality calling up such conflict in Lars. But something stopped her. She said calmly, "Why don't we go there now?"

"Get it over with," he said. Nor was he joking.

She walked ahead of him through the trees and got in her car. Over his shoulder he said, "I'll lead the way," and slammed the door of the Jaguar. Her mind a jumble of unanswered questions, Kristine followed him down the road.

At Brimnes they took the ferry to Ulvik, sea gulls dipping and diving in their wake. Ulvik more than fulfilled the glowing descriptions given it by the Americans, the houses with their red-tiled roofs dotting the hills, the white-capped mountains hovering behind. The waters of the fjord were crystal-clear.

Lars drove to a campsite that to her delight was on the shore. It seemed another good omen that the rain had subsided and the sky over the mountains was clearing. They set up their tents on the close-clipped grass under some trees, then Lars said, "I'm going for a walk—I'll be back in an hour."

She watched him wind his way through the trees and take the road toward the village. Because he had not asked her to go with him, she could only assume he was going to visit his wife's grave. Restlessly Kristine unpacked her gear, explored the campground and talked to a couple of German youths for half an hour, then

walked back to her tent. No sign of Lars. Impulsively—
he could hardly accuse her of following him, for he had
been gone for nearly an hour—she too set off toward
the village.

The rain had stopped, although the woods still smelled
richly of rotting leaves and damp earth. Poppies hung
heavy-headed in the gardens. She walked faster, realizing the exercise was what she needed. A dog trotted
past her, intent on its own errand. Ahead of her an
elderly man with stooped shoulders appeared from one
of the side streets and set off briskly down the road.
Watching him with only part of her attention, she decided that she, like the poppies, felt heavy-headed.

She stopped to sniff the deep red roses rambling over
the wrought-iron fence near the church, noticing that
the elderly man had gone into the churchyard. Perhaps
that was where Lars's wife was buried, she thought,
wishing Lars had seen fit to share the story of his marriage with her.

Then, shattering the somnolent silence of the summer
afternoon, she heard voices raised in anger, and with a
quiver along her nerves recognized one of the voices as
Lars's. It was coming from the churchyard.

Screened by the trees, she moved closer. Through the
wet leaves she saw Lars and the man with the stooped
shoulders standing on either side of a grave where flowers
grew in a bright tangle of color. She heard the man
sputter, in a British accent made more pronounced by
anger, "How dare you come back here?"

"I have a right to be here, Edward," Lars answered
levelly. But his fists were clenched at his sides and his
shoulders rigid.

"Eight years ago you forfeited any rights you had. I
told you then I never wanted to see you again, and
nothing since then has caused me to change my mind."
The man called Edward drew himself to his full height,

which was still several inches short of Lars's; yet the passion with which he spoke prevented him from being in any way a figure of ridicule. "Get out of here, Lars—I don't want you here."

"Edward, she was my wife..."

"You killed her! Her and the child."

"The child was my daughter!"

Kristine's fingers were gripping the fence so hard that the pattern on the wrought iron was imprinted on her flesh. She had never heard such agony in a man's voice before; that it should be Lars's agony knifed her to the very core of her being.

Edward leaned forward, his thin shoulders shaking. "I curse the day you ever met my beautiful Anna," he said venomously. "My wife—her mother—has never been the same since the day Anna died. And it was all your fault."

Lars said in a cracked voice, "I was young—and she went to the ski meet of her own choice——"

"She went because she couldn't stay away from you! She had to go, she was so afraid for your safety, so terrified each time that you were going to kill yourself on the slopes...I wish to God you had."

Lars's chest rose and fell. "Can't you find it in you to forgive me?" he said. "Anna, of all people, wouldn't want you harboring such anger and bitterness."

Edward struck out at Lars, a feeble gesture that nevertheless made Kristine wince. "I'll never forgive you—never!" he vowed. "And I never want to see you in Ulvik again."

She shrank back into the trees as Edward marched toward the gate. He passed within four feet of her, blind to anything but his own emotions. His face was mottled red, and his eyes, she saw to her deep distress, were filled with tears. His footsteps receded down the road.

Lars stood very still beside his wife's grave, his hands thrust in his pockets. For the first time Kristine noticed another plot beyond him, a smaller one covered with tiny blue-and-white flowers. The grave of his daughter, she thought painfully.

She understood now why Lars had not wanted to come to Ulvik. She also glimpsed why he had changed his mind: he had probably hoped that Edward, after all these years, might have forgiven him, and this hope had been worth the risk of coming here.

But Edward had not forgiven him. Nor, she was almost sure, had Lars forgiven himself.

Lars had told her nothing of all this; would not even have told her he was a widower had they not met Kevin in the bar. So the last thing she should do now was to intrude on a grief that was intensely private, much as she might want to. Soft-footed, Kristine edged along the fence until the church was out of sight.

She walked for half an hour and could not have told anyone afterward what she had seen. Then she headed back the way she had come, feeling as far from the peace the tourists had promised her as it was possible to feel. As she came around the corner of the churchyard, she saw that her timing could not have been worse, for Lars was just leaving through the gate.

He saw her immediately. He said in an ugly voice, "What are you doing here?"

He looked terrible, his eyes sunk in their sockets, the skin stretched tight across his cheekbones; with an immense effort Kristine kept her face impassive. She said straightforwardly, "I overheard you and Edward—I didn't mean to, it just happened that way."

"And now you just happened to be walking past when I'm leaving."

She raised her chin. "That was chance as well."

"Of course," he said with a sarcasm she deplored.

She walked closer to him. He held his ground, brushing away a branch that was hanging over his shoulder, droplets of water running down his arm. Like tears, she thought, and said quietly, "Tell me what happened, Lars."

"If you overheard Edward, you know what happened—I was responsible for the deaths of my wife and my daughter."

"That was Edward's version. I want yours."

"All right, I'll tell you," he said unpleasantly. "It's the only way I'll get you off my back, isn't it? What do you want to know, Kristine?"

She refused to back down. "What happened at the ski meet?"

He pulled a leaf from the branch and methodically started shredding it to pieces. "Anna hated risk. I didn't know that when I married her—I was only twenty-one, fresh out of university, stuffed with book knowledge and ready to take on the world. I was also an avid skier, and I made the national team the year I graduated, just before she and I met. Her father and mother had retired in Ulvik, and she was working in Oslo. She was beautiful and gentle as a spring rain and she loved me...so we got married. There was enough to keep me busy at Asgard and in between I skied every chance I got."

He yanked off another leaf. "She hated the ski meets—she thought I was going to get killed each time I left the gate. After every competition she would cry and beg me to stay home. But I couldn't. I needed the risk and the excitement and I couldn't understand why she was so afraid—I felt smothered by her fear. When she got pregnant she wouldn't risk going out on the slopes to watch, and so for a while everything was all right again. But once Elisabet was born Anna wept every time I left her, and so finally I told her I'd quit at the end of the season."

He was looking beyond Kristine, his eyes filled with memories. "She came to the closing meet, in the spring, Elisabet in a carrier on her back. She was happy, because I'd promised this was the last time and she knew I wouldn't go back on my word." Very carefully he ripped the leaf apart along the center vein. "There was a freak avalanche—maybe you remember hearing about it—over a hundred spectators were killed. Anna and Elisabet were among them. Their bodies were recovered two days later."

Dropping the torn leaf so that it fluttered to the ground, he brushed his hands down his sides. "Edward, as you heard, blamed me. He didn't need to—I was blaming myself enough for ten men. If I'd quit when she first asked me, they'd still be alive...but I didn't want to quit." He looked up, his eyes blank. "End of story."

Kristine could have said any number of things. That he had been very young. That he had been prepared to give up something he loved for his wife's sake. That he could scarcely be blamed for a freak accident. She said none of them. Nor did she try to touch him; she was almost sure that if she did he would strike her away as Edward had struck him. Instead she said, "Thank you for telling me...and I'm truly sorry."

The blankness in his eyes lifted briefly. "You are, aren't you?" he said. "You're very different from her, Kristine. I can't imagine Anna tackling a couple of thieves with a pair of nail scissors and a Swiss army knife."

"But when I tell you how afraid I am I remind you of her. That's what you meant by history repeating itself."

Although he nodded, the blank look was back on his face again. "Let's go back to the campsite," he said.

"I'm going to take off in the car for the rest of the day—I'm in a foul mood and I need to be alone."

"We could leave Ulvik now if you'd like."

"No...now that I'm here, I'd rather stay."

Fifteen minutes later he was gone. Kristine went swimming, explored the village, bought a few groceries and made her own supper. She went to bed at ten-thirty, lay awake for an hour listening for Lars, and woke up with a jerk at three in the morning. Peering through her mosquito netting, she saw the Jaguar parked on the grass beside her battered little car. So he was back.

She lay down and tried to sleep again, but her brain was going around in circles and she couldn't rid her mind of all that had happened the day before. Eventually she slid out of her sleeping bag and padded barefoot across the grass to the water's edge, where she sat down on a rock, wrapping her short cotton nightshirt around her knees for warmth. The sky had cleared, stars twinkling above the black line of the mountains; the new moon looked as though it had been painted on the sky as an afterthought.

Little waves were chuckling among the rocks. She listened to them, lost in thought, remembering Edward's corrosive accusations and Lars's plea for forgiveness, wishing there were some way she could help him, knowing there was not. She knew something else: for her to lie awake at night worrying about a man who two weeks ago had been a stranger was no longer travelling light. Whether she liked it or not, Lars had become a part of her life.

Under the night sky the surface of the water was a liquid black, shiny like obsidian. Then a gust of wind ruffled its surface and the waves gurgled and sloshed against the shore. If she went to visit her grandfather, even less would she be travelling light...

A hand fell on Kristine's shoulder. With a shriek of alarm she twisted round, nearly falling off the rock, her nightshirt rucked up above her knees.

Lars grabbed for her, his arms going hard around her body. "I thought you heard me coming—I said your name."

"I—I was miles away," she faltered. His forearm was against her breast and her knee was digging into his bare thigh; he was wearing nothing but a pair of shorts. She felt her heart begin to race, her eyes dark as the velvet sky. With a muffled groan Lars lowered his mouth to hers and kissed her.

Raw physical hunger streaked through her veins. This was what she had been craving ever since he had kissed her on the beach at Mandal. Except this time she would not run away.

He kissed her until she could scarcely breathe, and then his lips slid down her throat, finding the hollow at its base where the pulse throbbed under her skin. She said, torn between passion and reality, laughter warming her voice, "Lars, I don't want you to stop kissing me, but if we don't move very soon this rock is going to permanently cripple me."

"A minor detail," he murmured, taking her weight and edging her from the rock to the grass, then pushing the neckline of her shirt aside to smooth the long curve where her neck became her shoulder. As she ran her fingers through his hair, his hand closed over the swell of her breast.

The bittersweet ache spread through her whole body. He had raised his head, and it was as though she saw straight into his soul, his eyes as black and depthless as the waters of the fjord. "I want to make love to you— I'm not afraid any more," she whispered, simple words that carried a weight of meaning.

Each of them knew that under the thin nightshirt she was naked; and each of them was surrounded and held by the soft, seductive blackness of a summer night. Lars's arms tightened around her. Kristine waited for whatever he might do next, knowing she would make love with him on the damp grass under the stars and that nothing she had ever done in her twenty-three years could feel more right than that.

Then he loosened his hold and pulled her to her feet, keeping her hands clasped in his. He said, both his crooked smile and his accent very much in evidence, "We agreed we'd make that decision when we weren't in the same room, let alone in each other's arms. And there are too many memories for me here in Ulvik, Kris...I don't want to be with you for the first time in this place. Not here. Not yet."

"But soon."

He ran one finger along the curve of her cheek, down her throat to the tip of her breast, all the while keeping his eyes trained on the yearning in her face. "Yes. Very soon."

With attempted lightness she said, "I was having trouble sleeping—that's why I got up. I don't think you've helped matters at all."

He chuckled. "I'm not going to offer to hold your hand while you fall asleep—because we both know where that will lead."

Kristine had never made love before, so she was not at all sure where it would lead; she did know she wanted very badly to find out, and that for now she would have to wait. "Good night, then, Lars," she said. Resting her palms flat on his bare chest, feeling the roughness of hair and the heat of his skin, she reached up and kissed him on the mouth.

His response was to pull her hard against him, his hands roaming her body as if there were no tomorrow and no yesterday, only the present moment in all its passionate urgency. He was putting his mark on her, she thought dazedly, claiming her for his own, and wished fervently that they were anywhere but in Ulvik. Anywhere else, and she was almost sure Lars would not be thrusting her away as he now was.

His chest heaving, he said hoarsely, "So much for good intentions."

"We won't always be in Ulvik," Kristine said.

"I've never wanted a woman as I want you, I swear it."

Because she was beginning to suspect he had known as much loneliness in his life as she had in hers, her eyes unexpectedly filled with tears. Giving him a tiny smile, afraid to touch him again, she hurried across the grass to her tent and crawled in. A few moments later she heard him go to his. The waves chattered among the rocks, and the wind stirred the trees, and she couldn't sleep for wanting the man who was lying only a few feet away from her.

Night gave way to the rosy light of dawn. The birds began to sing, first one, then a whole chorus chirping away as though they had never experienced sunrise before. Kristine pulled her sleeping bag around her ears and shut her eyes for what felt like the fiftieth time. When she finally fell asleep, she dreamed that the ferry was sinking in the fjord and she along with it, and woke with a start. One of the other campers was gunning his motorbike, an uncouth roar that brought her fully awake.

She yanked on her swimsuit. She felt tired and out of sorts and sexually frustrated, she decided grumpily, unzipping her mosquito net and climbing out of her tent. Her frustration sharpened dramatically when she saw Lars walking back from the shore, water coating his body and dripping from his hair. He gave her a cheerful grin. "The water's great."

"I just hope it's good and cold," she said and walked past him with her gaze averted from his bare chest.

He called after her, "My brother has a cottage in Vetlefjord, and he's in Denmark for two weeks."

She turned, glaring at him. "How many hundreds of miles away is Vetlefjord?"

"We could probably get there tonight if the ferries cooperate."

"I got exactly four and a half hours' sleep last night— it's time we did something."

"It's a very nice cottage. With beds."

"One bed will do. And don't tell me I'm behaving like a spoiled brat—I know I am."

"Your eyes look green as a cat's when you're angry," Lars said.

He was openly laughing at her. Kristine said a couple of very pithy words that Andreas had taught her, and went for a swim. The water was cold, but not cold enough.

CHAPTER SEVEN

AFTER a leisurely breakfast Kristine and Lars packed up and left the campsite, and Kristine for one was not sorry to see the last of Ulvik.

The road was narrow and steep, winding through dense woods, and the Fiat's engine appeared to be overheating. Kristine kept a nervous eye on the gauge. The needle flickered back into the safe zone once she reached the top of the incline. This was not the place to have car trouble, she thought. If her car gave out, she'd be wholly dependent on Lars.

Not ready for that yet, Kristine?

No, I'm not, she answered herself, drew up behind the Jaguar and put on her right-hand indicator to join the main road. They were delayed several times because of military maneuvers involving heavy trucks and large numbers of uniformed young men, so by the time they arrived at the Gudvangen ferry a long line was ahead of them. The ferry docked. The line inched forward. Five cars ahead of the Jaguar, the ferry pulled up its ramp and drew away from the dock. Lars walked back to talk to her. "A two-hour wait for the next one," he said. "Want to go for a walk?"

The sun was high in the sky, its heat trapped by the gorge, and Kristine was feeling the effects of her disturbed night. "I think I'll try and catch up on my sleep," she yawned. "See you later."

"We may not make it to the cottage at this rate," he said tersely.

The decision to spend the night at the cottage had definitely not been made with her head, Kristine thought, and was not sure whether she was glad or sorry that they might not get there tonight. As Lars watched the changing expressions on her face, he added in a voice rough with emotion, "If I've never wanted a woman as I want you, I've also never felt as uncertain of a woman as I do of you."

Not knowing what to say to this, Kristine said nothing. He gave an impatient exclamation and disappeared through the ranks of parked cars. She folded her jacket into a pillow, leaned her head against the doorframe, and went to sleep.

An hour later she woke with a headache from the sun, which was blazing on the roof of her car. She climbed out, stretching the stiffness from her neck. The fjord shimmered in the heat, waterfalls plunging from the crest of the gorge in curtains of diaphanous white. But most of the day the gorge would be in deep shadow, she realized, and felt a premonition of the cold of winter shiver along her nerves.

From behind her a voice said, "Kristine... *c'est toi*?"

She recognized the voice immediately, for she had travelled with its owner for nearly five months. Her premonition dissipated itself and a smile was already on her face as she turned. "Philippe! You said you were coming to Norway, but I never expected to bump into you——"

He picked her up, whirled her around, put her down and kissed her on both cheeks. Laughing, he said, "Fate intended it to happen."

He still had his arms around her, and she had forgotten how handsome he was with his cherubic brown eyes and his long dark lashes. Logically she should feel the same tumult of longing that such an embrace with Lars would have awoken. In actuality she felt nothing but the pleasure of seeing an old friend. "Where are you going?" she asked. "Are you alone?"

But he was looking at her in puzzlement. "Something has changed," he said slowly. "You are not the same."

It was not the opportune time for her to see, over Philippe's quite muscular shoulder, that Lars was watching them. A Lars who looked, to put it mildly, displeased. She gabbled, "Well, I'm travelling with someone, you see. He's over there and his name is Lars—maybe that's why."

Philippe had accepted with reasonably good grace Kristine's insistence that he and she could be travelling companions but not lovers; but he was clearly not thrilled to think that another man might have succeeded where he had not. "A Norwegian?" he said, giving Lars an unfriendly look. "They're cold, Kristine—cold and cautious. They are too much in the snow and the ice. You don't want a Norwegian."

She was not about to tell him that she wanted this particular Norwegian very much. "Keep your voice down," she scolded. "He and I are friends, that's all."

"Why then does he look as if he wants to cut me in little pieces and feed me to the fishes?"

An unanswerable question. Kristine tugged at his sleeve. "Come on and I'll introduce you."

"Indeed," said Philippe, a martial light in his eye. "I 'ave to see if this Norwegian is good enough for you."

Philippe's accent, like Lars's, deteriorated under stress. If she had not had a headache, and if she were indeed Lars's lover, as Philippe obviously thought she was, this scene might not have been so farcical. Kristine marched Philippe up to Lars, smiled at Lars determinedly, and said, "Lars, you've heard me speak of Philippe—he's the one who taught me the trick with the nail scissors. Philippe Aubin, Lars Bronstad."

Philippe bowed stiffly from the waist. His brown hair curled to the neckline of his T-shirt, and the toes were out of his sneakers. He said pugnaciously, "Kristine and I 'ave travel many months together. She is a very fine person."

Lars said smoothly, "I couldn't agree more."

"How then did you meet her?" Philippe asked suspiciously.

Kristine poured out the story of the two clowns in the park. Philippe's response was, she supposed, predictable. "Because of what I have teach you, you do not need the rescue," he said.

There was a diabolical gleam of amusement in Lars's eyes. In a gesture that openly laid claim to Kristine, he put his arm around her shoulders and said, "I was very glad she knew how to defend herself—you taught her well."

Philippe was quite astute enough to discern the tremor of pleasure Kristine felt from Lars's embrace. He drew himself to his full height. "She is my friend," he announced.

"As she is mine," Lars responded, an edge to his voice.

This was ludicrous, thought Kristine. Philippe could have been a knight of old flinging his gauntlet in his rival's face, a gauntlet Lars looked quite prepared to pick up. "I'm really glad to see you again, Philippe," she said sincerely. "I hope you and Lars can be friends."

Philippe stopped scowling at Lars and gave her his most charming smile. "We 'ave many memories to talk about," he said. "I am with Daniel and Suzette—remember them? Tonight we camp at Kaupanger, the other end of this ferry trip, and we 'ave steak we buy from a farmer for supper—you will both join us, please?" His eyes flicked a challenge at Lars, sharp as a sword's parry.

If they ate supper with Philippe, who somehow always managed to travel with more than his share of wine and

beer, she and Lars would never make it to the cottage.
She said quickly, "That would be fun—wouldn't it,
Lars?"

"*Bien*," said Philippe, not waiting for her companion's response. "We meet you there...'ere comes the
ferry."

As the ferry gave a blast on its whistle, the noise echoed
down the gorge. Kristine jumped, Philippe gave Lars a
self-satisfied smile and walked toward the back of the
line, and Lars said ferociously, "Do you or do you not
want to go to bed with me, Kristine Kleiven?"

"I never went to bed with Philippe," she said
obliquely.

"Not because he didn't want to!"

"*I* didn't want to."

"So why am I different?"

"That's the sixty-four-dollar question," she retorted
in exasperation. "But you said yourself we should make
up our minds when we're not together, and whenever
that happens I get cold feet."

"Tomorrow night we're going to my brother's
cottage," Lars grated. "There are two bedrooms and a
hammock, and you can decide when we get there where
you and your cold feet want to sleep—because I'm
damned if I'm taking anyone into my bed who doesn't
want to be there."

The gauntlet had been thrown in her face. She said
mutinously, "If we stand here arguing we're going to
miss the ferry."

"We can't risk that—we'd miss this wonderful dinner
with Philippe."

"You're jealous," Kristine said in amazement. "But
you don't have to——"

"I'm confused, I'm angry and I'm sexually frustrated," Lars said succinctly. "If you want to add jealous
to that, feel free."

"The other cars are driving off so we'd better go," she said, stepping to the side of the road.

Lars grabbed her by the shoulder, kissed her hard on the lips, and tramped off toward his car. Kristine stood with her mouth open, the kiss having driven any intelligent response from her mind, and then hurried after him. She was glad she didn't know anyone else in the lineup; there were advantages to being in a foreign country. Certainly her four brothers, who thought of her as even-tempered and very much in control of her life, would not recognize her now.

The dinner with Philippe was not at all the ordeal that Kristine had envisaged, because Lars set himself out to be friendly and the wine mellowed Philippe. The steaks were excellent, and afterward they sang around the campfire accompanied by Suzette on the guitar. They then went to their separate sleeping bags.

Lars had not kissed Kristine good-night. Neither had he paid any more attention to her all evening than he had to Philippe, Daniel or Suzette; plainly Philippe was not quite so sure that she and Lars were lovers. Doing up her tent flap, Kristine also decided Lars had meant every word he'd said this afternoon. The choice of beds at the cottage would be hers, and hers alone.

If they made love, Lars was not the kind of man to conveniently disappear afterward. How was she to know what she would feel for him once they were lovers? Perhaps sharing his bed would mean she couldn't travel light ever again.

Is that what she wanted? To travel with Lars at her side?

Could one man undo the lessons of a lifetime?

Kristine, Lars and Philippe parted company very amiably the next morning. It was to be another hot day, Kristine thought, glancing up at the pale blue sky where the sun already blazed white. "I may have to drive slowly," she said to Lars as they packed the last of their gear. "My car was overheating a bit yesterday."

"We could have it checked in Balestrand."

Mechanics cost money. "We don't have much farther to go to Fjaerland, do we? Probably someone in my family could fix it for me," she said hopefully. Although, for all she knew, her family might not let her past the door.

"So you've definitely decided to go and see your grandfather?"

"I guess I have." She sighed. "I want to know why my father left home twenty years ago, and he'll never tell me. I have this memory—I think from the first year we were in Canada, so I'd have been very young—of a letter arriving with pretty stamps on it and a red-and-blue border on the envelope, and of my father tearing it to pieces and my mother crying as if her heart would break...she always hated Canada. She still does. Her only contact with home is the Christmas card she sends to Harald's mother."

In the first sign of gentleness she had seen in Lars for what felt like a long time, his face softened. "Then I think you're right to go. I can see it's not easy, Kristine."

"Nothing seems very easy," she burst out. "I know I'm up and down like a yo-yo where you're concerned, Lars. Right now when you look at me like that I'd make love with you in the back seat of the car...and then as soon as you're out of sight round a bend in the road I start worrying again—it's crazy!"

He said flatly, "Because of what's happened in your life you worked out a certain way to survive, which served you well. But now you're having to decide if that's the way you want to live for the rest of your life. I want you to change—change is always frightening. And the choice is yours."

"All we're going to do is make love," she cried. "That doesn't have to change my whole life!"

His voice tempered like a steel blade, he said, "You might find it does."

She flung her haversack in the back seat and slammed the door. "Let's go," she said irritably.

"Why don't you go first? That way if you have car trouble I'm right behind you." He spread the map on the hood of her car, his finger tracing their route.

Kristine remembered how his hand had held the curve of her breast and stared blankly at the narrow red lines on the map, where the yellow of the land was split by fingers of blue. What am I going to do? she thought. What in heaven's name am I going to do?

"We take this ferry across the fjord," Lars concluded. "Then we turn north again."

"Fine," said Kristine, scurried around her car and started the engine. As smoothly as if it were a Jaguar, her little car drove out of the campsite.

The scenery was, as always, breathtaking. They drove along the shores of the fjord, which were bordered by mountains topped with blindingly white glaciers. Pink clover, purple knapweed and yellow daisies spattered the fields as though an artist had gone wild with her brush. The next ferry took them across waters of a dazzling blue.

But as they started driving again Kristine soon found herself climbing steeply. Trees crowded the narrow road on either side, parting occasionally to allow unnerving glimpses of the trail far below, winding like a gray snake up the side of the mountain. She had heard of hairpin turns; perhaps Norwegians invented the term, she thought wryly, keeping a worried eye on the temperature gauge.

It was not up to the danger zone yet. Surely she'd make it safely to Fjaerland. And surely she'd find a welcome there after all these years. Even if her grandfather had shown her father the door he'd still be pleased to see his Canadian granddaughter. Of course he would.

The car groaned up the hill. She had already passed several of the triangular road signs warning of zigzags; Lars, who was keeping a careful distance behind her, was often out of sight. The Jaguar, she was quite sure, could swallow this mountain trail in a single gulp.

Then Kristine saw a new sign, a black triangle within the red one, and as she was working out that it must mean a sharp decline she arrived at the top of the mountain. The view was stupendous. For a fatal two or three moments she drank in the sinuous curves of the road far below and the faraway glitter of sun on the stream in the valley. Heaving mountain ranges stretched as far as she could see, their lower slopes clad in myriad shades of green. Then she brought her attention back to the road and braked sharply for the turn.

Nothing happened.

Her breath paralyzed in her throat, Kristine frantically pumped the brake, and with a kind of horrified fascination saw the first curve in the road rush toward her. Even though she had the presence of mind to gear down she took the turn much too fast, her tires squealing on the tarmac. A car laboring up the slope blasted its horn at her.

No matter how hard she pushed, the brake pedal went straight to the floor with no resistance. In a clash of gears Kristine shifted to second and felt the rubber momentarily grasp the road, the car bucking like a bad-tempered horse.

The next turn presented her with a sickening view of tumbled rocks disappearing into nothingness on her left. The tires crunched in the gravel shoulder and with a tiny

sound of sheer terror she ground the gearshift into first
and pulled hard on the hand brake.

The car slewed sideways. The drop surged toward her.
Kristine wrestled with the wheel, desperately aiming for
the opposite bank, and by some miracle the Fiat responded. She saw rocks and the slim white trunk of a
birch tree rushing at her. Clutching the wheel as though
it were a lifeline, she thought with total clarity what a
fool she'd been not to have made love with Lars. Then
she closed her eyes for the crash.

The noise was deafening—the hideous scrape of metal
on stone, the shattering of glass, the whine and screech
as the car body buckled around her. And then, dramatically, silence.

Birch leaves were brushing her nose through the gap
where the windshield had been. Kristine raised a hand
to push them away and saw blood on her wrist. I'm
bleeding, she thought. So I must be alive.

But the words made no impact; it all could have been
happening to someone else. From a long way away she
saw a face appear in her window, a man's face as familiar to her as her own. Lars. Of course, he had been following her. Although he looked awful, she thought
detachedly. Dead white under his tan. How odd. She
wouldn't have thought you could look white under a tan.

He was saying something. She frowned, trying to concentrate. He seemed to be asking if she was hurt. What
a silly question, she thought. How did she know?

Then he was wrenching her door open. It squealed
horribly, just as if the crash were happening all over
again. She gave a whimper of fear and tried to strike
him away.

He reached around and unbuckled her seat belt. Then,
with exquisite gentleness coupled with an underlying
haste she could not understand, he was easing her out
of her seat. Pain stabbed her at wrist and knee. Her

head flopped against his chest as she breathed in shallow gasps that seemed to come from somewhere outside her.

Lars was running up the slope away from the car. He was jolting her unforgivably, each step sending arrows of pain shooting along her limbs. She mumbled a protest.

From behind them came a sound like a miniature clap of thunder. Lars froze to the spot. Then, slowly, he turned, and Kristine saw with numb disbelief that the hood of her little car was enveloped in flames, bright orange flames sending up billows of thick black smoke.

Lars's body sagged. "Thank God I was so close behind you," he said hoarsely, and tightened his arms around her, his face resting on her hair.

Past his shoulder she could see the Jaguar parked by the side of the road. Another car that had come around the bend had jammed itself into the space behind it. The driver was running toward them, shouting something.

It was all too much. Kristine closed her eyes, her last recollection the heavy pounding of Lars's heart beneath her cheek.

Kristine was in a room she had never seen before. A very pleasant room, she thought in puzzlement. It was painted a soft pink with white trim, and golden light was pouring in the tall window, carrying with it the fragrance of roses.

The cottage? Surely not. No cottage she had ever been in had had such a high ceiling or such an air of faded elegance.

She was lying flat on her back in bed, a double bed with crisp white sheets that smelled of summer breezes and sunshine. Her arms were on top of the covers, one wrist bandaged. Her head hurt. She moved her limbs and discovered that her knees and her elbows hurt, too. Then the door opened and Lars came in. "Is this the cottage?" she croaked.

"You're awake!" he exclaimed, crossing the room in three quick strides and sitting very carefully on the edge of the bed. "They stuffed you full of painkillers at the hospital. But the doctor said you should wake up before evening."

"Doctor? I——" Her eyes suddenly widened as memory rushed back. "The car—the brakes failed. Oh, Lars, I was so scared, I thought I was going to die——"

She pushed herself up, blindly reaching out for him. He took her in his arms, holding her as she stammered out the terrible fear of those last few moments before the accident. Then she suddenly raised her head, meeting his eyes. "You saved my life," she whispered. "I remember now—the engine exploded, didn't it? You were afraid that was going to happen—that's why you were in such a hurry to get me out of the car..." A tremor racked her body. "Lars, how can I ever thank you?"

"I don't need thanks," he said in a voice husky with emotion. "Having you here is thanks enough."

She scarcely heard, because another memory had surfaced. She blurted it out. "Do you know what was the last thing I thought before I ran into the cliff? I thought what a fool I'd been not to have made love with you. I—I was afraid it was going to be too late."

Her eyes filled with easy tears. Lars said cogently, "You're supposed to be resting. And we aren't going to be doing anything as active as making love for several nights, *elskling*—you've got cuts on your knees and wrist and you're covered with bruises. But tomorrow we'll drive as far as the cottage and you can recuperate there."

"Where are we now?"

"The best hotel in Balestrand. And I want no arguments about money."

Incredibly she managed a laugh. "You're quite safe, I don't have the energy to argue...is it evening already?" He nodded. "Will you be here tonight?"

"The staff's going to bring in a cot so I can sleep in the same room. And don't worry about your things—the fellow who came along behind us got your backpack out of the trunk."

He lowered her to the pillows, the expression on his face filling her with a wild, unreasoning happiness. She said, knowing her words for the truth, "Lars, you redeemed something today. You weren't able to save Anna or Elisabet...but you did save my life, and that has to count for something."

He was playing with her fingers. He said roughly, "When I came round the bend and saw your car smashed into the cliff, I thought I'd lost you too. I don't think I could have borne that, Kristine."

She said with all the energy she could muster, "You don't have to—because you saved my life."

Drained by the effort those few words had taken, she lay back on the pillows. He had saved her life. Did that give him a claim on her? If so, she would never travel light again, whether she was with him or not.

CHAPTER EIGHT

FOUR days later Kristine was swinging gently back and forth in the hammock on the front balcony of the mountain cottage that belonged to Lars's brother. The cuts on her knees were healing, although her bruises were now an unbecoming, jaundiced shade of yellow. Today she had gone swimming in the lake behind the cottage for the first time since the accident, Lars never straying far from her side.

He was inside cooking dinner. He liked to cook, she had discovered, although he had a dislike of recipes, preferring to improvise. The results were always interesting and almost always edible.

For the last four days, he could have been one of her brothers.

The words had come unbidden to her mind. She gazed at the horizon, where the glacier called Voggebreen reflected the rays of the sun, and played with the words. Lars had fed her and changed the dressings on her knees and washed the horrible scent of smoke from her clothes. Two nights ago he had held her hand when she had woken from a horrifying dream of being enveloped in fire. And all this he had done as impersonally as if she were a chance-met stranger.

At first she had been too tired to care; the shock of the accident had so exhausted her normally buoyant stock of energy that she could not have handled any emotional demands from him. But she was feeling better now. Much better. So much so that his impartial kindness, his casual conversations were beginning to irk her beyond belief.

Perhaps he had changed his mind. Perhaps he didn't want to make love with her any more.

Yet even as she formed the words her instincts told her they could not possibly be true. Lars was as steady as a rock, as steady as the granite boulders that surrounded the cottage. So if she assumed he still wanted her he was holding back for a reason, and the most logical reason was her injuries.

She looked down at her knees, scabbed and bruised and far from pretty. She was certainly no magazine pin-up. Was that the problem? He didn't like her looking less than perfect?

Somehow she didn't think that was true either. So perhaps the reason lay in the conversation—or rather, argument—they had had while they were waiting for the Gudvangen ferry. Lars had said words to the effect that he wouldn't force her. She could choose whether she wanted to make love with him. And she could choose when.

She rubbed her elbow. She had three stitches in one of her cuts and they itched. She would have much preferred not to look like a patchwork quilt the first time she made love with Lars. But she was tired of waiting. There had been integrity in the agony of regret that had seized her in the moment before the accident—integrity and truth. And thanks to Lars she had been given a second chance.

She extricated herself from the hammock, feeling various twinges from muscles and tendons that were still healing. Wandering into the kitchen, she gave Lars a bright smile. "How long before dinner?"

He was peering rather dubiously at a sauce he was stirring. "Half an hour," he said abstractedly.

He was wearing shorts and a vest top, minimal garments that strengthened her resolve. "I think I'll have a shower," she said.

His attention was solely on the saucepan. "Go ahead."

Her eyes narrowed. I'm going to make you sit up and take notice, she thought, or I'm not worthy to be called a woman.

Nose in the air, she pivoted and headed for the bathroom. She showered and shampooed her hair, wrapped a towel around herself, went back to her bedroom and closed the door. Then she settled down to some serious work.

Her hair was growing; she dried it briskly, encouraging its natural wave until it stood around her head in a froth of curls, thereby covering most of the bruises on her forehead. She spent twenty minutes making up her face. Her dark sweep of lashes and dramatically heightened eyes, while they did not totally mask the scratches on her cheek, certainly distracted from them. She then slid her naked body into the sea green jumpsuit that Gianetta had given her, painted her fingernails and toenails, and buckled her blue sandals on her feet.

There was a full-length mirror on the back of the wardrobe door. While the jumpsuit hid the deplorable state of her knees, it hid very little else, she thought, wondering if she was going to have the courage to walk into the kitchen dressed like this.

He probably won't even notice. He'll be too busy stirring the sauce.

Right on cue, Lars called down the hall, "Are you out of the shower, Kristine? Dinner's ready."

And so was she. She took a moment to practice a seductive smile in the mirror, then swayed toward the kitchen in her high heels, trying to ignore how they accentuated her various aches and pains. Lars had set the teak table in the alcove overlooking the serried mountains and the lake; she took the candles from the mantelpiece, lit them, and put them on the table, then quickly went out on the deck to pick one of the sweetly scented

Rugosa roses that grew wild around the cottage. As she came back in, Lars was carrying a casserole dish in from the kitchen. He took one look at her, put the dish down on the table, and said, "My God."

She was holding the deep pink rose to her breast. The turquoise fabric clung to the curves of her body, baring the creamy skin of her shoulders. Her cheeks were as pink as the rose, her eyes very blue, looking straight at him with a mixture of bravado, pride and intense shyness.

Slowly Lars pulled off the oven mitts. "The casserole will keep hot for a few minutes," he said. "You don't mind waiting, do you, Kristine?"

She shook her head, wondering what he was going to do and wishing she had the courage to produce the seductive smile she had practiced in front of the mirror. He strode down the hall and vanished into his room. Kristine carried the casserole back into the kitchen and put it in the oven, opened the bottle of chilled white wine that was sitting on the counter, and poured herself a glass. From down the hall she heard the hiss of the shower.

Her heart was thumping in her chest. She had certainly gotten his attention, she thought, and put the rose in a vase on the table. Her eyes strayed through the window and past the hammock. Mountains were supposed to restore a sense of proportion, weren't they? Maybe if she stared at them very hard she wouldn't feel so nervous.

The soft pad of Lars's steps came down the hall. She turned, feeling very much at bay, and saw that he had changed into a pair of light suede pants and a full-sleeved, boldly patterned shirt. His hair was still damp. He stepped close to her, pressed his lips to her palm, and said softly, "I can never anticipate what you're going to do next."

Her nipples had hardened under the thin fabric. He added even more softly, "There is time, Kristine . . . we have all night."

She stroked his hair back from his forehead and saw passion flare in his eyes. "So you do still want me," she said.

"You've doubted that?"

"I've wondered."

"Then I'm better at hiding my feelings than I thought. And I wanted you to be very sure."

"I'm sure." She gave him a brilliant smile, unaware that it was infinitely more seductive than the one she had practiced in the mirror. "Shall I pour you a glass of wine?"

"In a moment," he said, and kissed her.

It was a lingering, sensual kiss that made her clutch at him for support, her body melting into his, her lips responding with a generosity that was instinctive. As he raised his head, his eyes churning with emotion, she murmured, "If you keep that up I won't be able to breathe, let alone eat."

His smile was open to her in a way that she cherished. "This is the first time for you—I want you never to forget tonight."

Never was a long time. As Kristine felt all the old inhibitions entangle her, Lars said strongly, "You have nothing to fear from me, I promise you."

She poured his wine, raised her glass, and said, knowing she was putting her trust in him, "To us."

They ate by candlelight as the sun sank toward the mountain peaks; they talked and kissed and held hands; and as the slow moments passed Kristine gained an inkling of the force of will that Lars had exerted over the last few days to hide his passionate need of her. Then he put on some music, and they danced, in the small space, her arms looped around his neck and her breasts rubbing the hard wall of his chest, his hands smoothing the curves of her waist and hips. And all the while her desire throbbed through her veins.

When he swung her into his arms and carried her to his room, Kristine was almost faint with longing. She had long ago kicked off her sandals; as he hauled his shirt over his head, she twisted to reach the back zip on her jumpsuit, trying to ignore her bruised ribs. Lars said quickly, "Here, let me."

Against her back she felt the warm slide of his fingers down her spine. Then he was easing the straps from her shoulders, and his hands came around her body to cup the swell of her breasts. She cried out her delight, arching against him, then blindly seeking his mouth. He kissed her again and again, hard kisses that set his seal on her, and in between he murmured her name in a fierce litany of passion.

The jumpsuit slithered down Kristine's hips. She stepped out of it and turned gladly into his arms, proud in her nakedness, and in his face saw wonderment, primitive hunger, and another emotion, a far more complex and daunting emotion. "Lars—what's wrong?"

He shook his head, drinking in every detail of her body. "You're so beautiful," he said in a voice she had never heard him use before. "And so generous and brave with your beauty."

Somehow she knew he was talking about his dead wife as much as about her, and knew too that this was not the time to ask. "It's easy to give to someone who wants to receive," she said, and reached for the waistband of his pants.

He was naked beneath them, naked and fully aroused. As briefly she faltered, he lifted her on the bed and lay down beside her. "I'll be as gentle with you as I know how, *elskling*."

Taking his face in her hands, she told the simple truth. "There's nowhere I would rather be than here with you, Lars." Then she kissed him with a seductiveness all the more powerful for being quite untutored.

For the next few minutes, minutes that were out of time, Lars left the initiative to her. Her tongue danced with his. Her hands clasped the hard bone of his shoulders, tangled themselves in the hair on his chest, and caressed the strong curve of his rib cage. As her lips slid down his throat, tasting his skin, teasing and probing, her hips instinctively pressed against his in a beguiling mixture of innocence and ageless knowledge.

He gasped her name, his face contorted. In sudden bewilderment, she said, "Don't you like that? Shouldn't I——?"

"Of course I like it. But I'm so afraid of hurting you," he said harshly.

Drawing on all the wisdom of her twenty-three years, knowing he was holding back although not at all sure why, Kristine said, "You won't hurt me, Lars—you couldn't." Then, intuitively, she guided his hand to her breast.

Something broke in him, something that had been confined for too long and now was free. Stroking the pale gleam of her skin, he brought his mouth to the swelling flesh, and as she cried out with the startling, incredible sweetness of his touch he drew her close to the length of his body.

Giving herself over to sensations as new as the dawn and as acute as lightning, Kristine matched him kiss for kiss, caress for caress. Then he found between her thighs the warm, wet petals of flesh that told him without words how ready she was to receive him. Again she whimpered with pleasure, wrapping her legs around his, unashamedly gathering him in. But even in the midst of a hunger so desperate that she could scarcely breathe she was aware of the care and sensitivity with which Lars took her. His control did not come without cost, she saw that too, and by his very restraint was bound to him more closely.

He was watching her face, where the remnants of fear, a flash of pain, and then an instinctive wonder chased each other vividly across her features. She suddenly grasped him by the hips, pulling him into her. "Now, Lars," she said, "*now*..." and knew she had never been more fully herself than in this moment when a man was entering her body in an intimacy wholly new to her. Then she stopped thinking altogether, tumbling into a whirlwind of tumultuous emotion, her broken cries and Lars's mating in the storm's heart. And finally, in that heart, she found utter silence and an immense peace.

She was lying on her back, Lars covering her, his breathing slowly returning to normal, his face hidden in her shoulder. The stitches on her elbow were jammed into the sheet. Yet she hated to break the silence, to return to the world of mundane reality.

Against her throat he murmured, "Kristine, are you all right?"

She gave an incredulous chuckle. "All right? I should say so! Why didn't you tell me how wonderful this would be?"

He glanced up, laughter lurking in his eyes. "Didn't want to brag."

Her chuckle turned into a full-fledged laugh. "I probably wouldn't have believed you anyway... you've got to move, the stitches in my elbow are hurting."

He lifted his weight from her, his torso a taut curve. "As long as it's only your elbow," he said.

She flushed a bright pink. "I don't know why I'm blushing," she said crossly, "after all that we just did." Glancing at him through her mascaraed lashes, she added doubtfully, "Was it wonderful for you too?"

He collapsed beside her, drawing her around to face him. "Couldn't you tell?"

"I have no basis for comparison," she said, wrinkling her nose at him. "Plus I was rather caught up in all that was going on."

The smile died from his face. "Yes, it was wonderful for me too." He hesitated, playing with a strand of her hair. "I don't even know if I should say this, Kris...but I want you to understand. I loved Anna when I married her, and she was sweet and gentle and a loving mother to Elisabet. But she was frightened by anything that she sensed was beyond her control—a ski slope, love-making—anything wild and exuberant and joyous." He moved his shoulders restlessly, avoiding Kristine's eyes. "So I became tame and domesticated. I kept my true self under wraps, giving her in bed only what she wanted because the alternative was to frighten her, and I hated to do that."

Kristine lay still, his few words making clear to her how hard-won was his willpower and his self-control. "That's why you needed the ski meets—they were the only outlet you had."

"I suppose you're right."

Her heart clenched with compassion. She said gently, "You were as afraid as I was of making love, weren't you?"

"I needn't have been. Because you're generous and brave and passionate. I watched you putting your trust in me—that was an immeasurable gift, *min kjaere elskling*."

Not sure which was the greater intimacy, his love-making or the disclosure of what his marriage had been like, she said fiercely, "I want you to be yourself with me, Lars. Never less than who you are—I couldn't bear that."

He smiled into her eyes. "I was myself. And next time I'll be even freer because I won't be afraid of hurting you, and you'll be even wilder because you won't be going into the unknown."

She gave a shaky chuckle, widening her eyes in mock amazement. "Next time? That's like planning dinner when you've only just eaten lunch."

"We could get up and wash the dishes first," he teased.

"Oh, no," said Kristine, snuggling closer to him and kissing the hollow at the base of his throat, certain that she would recognize the flavor of his skin until the day she died. "I like being right where I am—you're stuck with me for now."

"Have you ever slept with a man before—in the literal sense of the word?"

"Nope."

"We could try that, too."

"I like that idea much better than cleaning up the kitchen," she said with a contented sigh, although she was quite sure she'd never sleep with Lars so disturbingly and fascinatingly close to her. She nestled her cheek into his chest, rested her hand on the hard jut of his hipbone, and closed her eyes.

When next she opened them, it was daylight. She blinked. Her field of vision was an expanse of tanned chest; her legs were entwined with a man's thighs, and the man was quite definitely in the mood for seduction. She said naughtily, "What, no cup of coffee in bed?"

"That comes later," Lars growled. "Kiss me."

"The masterful approach," she giggled, and stretched as sinuously as a cat.

"Do that again and you're in trouble."

So Kristine did it again, and as Lars abandoned his self-control and she began to put to use all her newfound knowledge she forgot about her morning coffee.

*　　*　　*

A week passed, a week as idyllic as a honeymoon. Kristine sang in the shower and on the hammock and practiced her Norwegian, and the last of her bruises disappeared. Lars cooked some inspired meals, repaired the diving board at the lake, and laughed more than she had ever heard him laugh before.

Every day they made love—sometimes with a wildness and wantonness Kristine would not have thought herself capable of, sometimes in an intense and utter silence; sometimes in daylight, sometimes by the flickering yellow glow of a candle. As she lay in the hammock on their eleventh day at the cottage listening to Lars pounding nails in the wharf, she knew she would never forget this place, or the man who had initiated her into the wonders of lovemaking. Never.

She had learned a lot about Lars in a very short time. Because she had already known something of the serious side of his character, it was a delight to watch him play the fool, to hear him match her joke for joke until she was choking with laughter. They had fun together, she thought. The kind of fun that she was almost sure her parents had never had.

Furthermore, she could visibly watch him throwing off the shackles of the past, both in bed and out, and with a strange sense of humility knew that she made him happy. She could not doubt it; it showed all over him.

She also knew more of the fabric of his life. Last night they had lingered over dinner, listening to the rain drum on the roof, the mountains obscured, their world shrunk to the immediate circle of rocks, grass, and drenched rosebushes around the veranda. "Tell me what you do," she had requested. "You used to ski, and you've been looking after your grandmother's affairs—there must be more."

He had stared into his glass, where the candle flame lit a ruby glow in the wine. "I'd always wanted to take my pilot's license," he'd said. "After Anna and Elisabet died I took lessons, and when I'd clocked enough hours I went overseas and got a job with a private company that flew in emergency supplies to war refugees and drought victims. When civil wars were involved, as they often were, it could be dangerous, and that suited me fine. I never took unnecessary risks with the crew or the plane, but if we'd been shot down I don't suppose I would have minded that much."

"When I first met you I thought you were a man-about-town waiting for his inheritance," Kristine had confessed. "I couldn't have been more wrong."

"Then I was offered a job with an engineering firm that specialized in Third World development, realistic stuff with a chance of making lasting improvements. From Malaysia I went to Brazil, and I was on my last week of a project there when Bestemor had a slight stroke. So I came home. A month later I met you."

"Will you go back to Brazil?"

"There's a UN job in the offing that I've applied for. A lot of travel." He had looked straight at her and said, unsmiling, "You'd like that, Kristine."

She'd had no idea what he meant. Suddenly edgy, because she liked things just the way they were and wanted no changes, she had pushed back her chair. "I picked enough wild strawberries this afternoon for dessert. Do you want some?"

"You're running away again."

"I want to live in the present for now, that's all."

"Some time we have to talk about the future," Lars had said, his gray blue eyes impaling her.

"But not yet. Not now," she had retorted, and had made her escape to the kitchen and the strawberries ...

Thoughtfully Kristine reached down with one foot and gave the hammock a push. That conversation had been last night. Was she being overly sensitive to imagine that it had changed something between her and Lars? That there had been strain between them today where the day before there had been only harmony?

She didn't want to think about the future, whatever that highly amorphous term might mean. The present was more than enough. They would have to leave the cottage in a day or two anyway, because Lars's brother wanted it for the weekend.

Fjaerland, she thought. I have to go to Fjaerland first. Once I know how I stand with my grandfather, I'll know better what to do. Because if he doesn't want anything to do with me I'll have to go back to Oslo. And Oslo raises a whole host of problems. I don't have a car, my money's running low, and I don't want to live off Lars.

While Lars had dealt with the wreckage of her car and the insurance claim, she was not very hopeful that the insurance company would give her any more money than the cost of one good meal in Oslo. She'd have to get a job soon. Or go home.

Attacked by a pang of homesickness, Kristine remembered the kitchen in the old farmhouse where she had grown up, the worn softwood floor and the red geraniums she had grown every winter in the bay window. She should go home. Settle down and go to university and study languages, so she could get a decent job overseas instead of having to depend on whatever came along.

The ring of hammer on nail had ceased. She saw Lars coming up the path toward her, a tall, long-limbed man who moved with unconscious grace, his blond head and blue eyes achingly familiar to her. If she went back to Canada she would miss him, she thought with a sharp clench in her belly. Miss him horribly.

Not wanting to follow this train of thought, she waited for him to reach the deck. "Lars," she said bluntly, "will you take me to Fjaerland?"

The hammer he was carrying dropped to the deck with a clatter. He bent to pick it up. Hunkered down near the hammock, his eyes on a level with hers, he said guardedly, "When?"

"Tomorrow?"

"We don't have to leave until the day after."

She picked at the tightly woven twine. "I need to know whether my grandfather will see me or not."

"And what if he invites you to stay for a month? Do I say a nice polite goodbye and drive back to Oslo as if these past few days had never happened?"

"Don't be angry! This has been wonderful, Lars, but it has to end and I have to go to Fjaerland, you must see that——"

"I see a lot," he said grimly, thwacking the nearest chunk of granite with the hammer so that sparks flew. "Yes, I'll take you to Fjaerland. No, I won't promise to drive back to Oslo as soon as I become an inconvenience to you."

"Stop it," she cried. "You're putting the worst possible interpretation on what I'm trying to say. We're *friends*! Of course I don't want you to disappear——"

With dangerous calm he said, "We're lovers, Kristine."

"All right, so we're lovers! But your brother's coming back and I have to go to Fjaerland . . . and we're having our first fight in nearly two weeks," she wailed.

"A new record," he murmured, caught hold of her and kissed her very comprehensively. The hammock gave an alarming lurch, and Kristine, beguiled, said, "We've never done it in a hammock before."

As he kissed her again, she realized thankfully that the future was settled for the next twenty-four hours. Tomorrow Lars would take her to Fjaerland. Beyond that, for now, she did not want to go.

And then she stopped thinking altogether.

CHAPTER NINE

KRISTINE fell instantly in love with Fjaerland. She and Lars had travelled there by ferry along the narrow fjord that bore the name of the village. The flanks of the fjord were furred with trees, the occasional farm sprawling halfway up the slope. Above the farms lurked the hard-edged mountains, where the white of the glaciers and the white of the clouds were one. The village itself was near the head of the fjord, the water silty from runoff from the great glacier called Supphellebreen.

Although the wooden houses and red barns of the village and the old-fashioned fishing sloops moored off-shore enchanted her, beneath Kristine's pleasure, like a dark thread, ran the knowledge that twenty years ago her father had left here in anger. Romanticize the sheer beauty of the village as she might, all the human emotions resided here as anywhere else. And some of those emotions were destructive.

Her grandfather lived near the glacier, so Lars found out by questioning an old man at the ferry dock. They set off, following the course of the river that ran from the glacier to the fjord, Lars keeping track of the farms that they passed. "It should be the next one," he said finally. "A yellow house, the old man said."

The yellow house was set partway up the hill, surrounded by a cluster of barns and sheds; it was also, Kristine saw to her dismay, surrounded by a number of cars. "Are you sure that's it?" she said nervously.

"It has to be. Looks like they're having a party...want to come back later?"

It had required all her courage to come this far. The thought of waiting until tomorrow was more than she could contemplate. "I know it's taken me nearly two years to get here," she said, "but now that I'm here I have to go in."

Lars turned up the driveway. The house was as charming as the rest of Fjaerland, its facade decorated with yellow-and-white fretwork, roses rambling untidily over the old stone foundations. There was no one in sight. Kristine checked her watch. "We're too early for dinner—what if something's wrong, Lars?"

"We'll leave," he said with comforting brevity, parking in the shade of the house.

She took a deep breath. "I wish I wasn't so scared," she muttered, and got out of the car.

The fragrance of the roses reached out to her in welcome. A cow was bawling in the field, and swallows chittered high above the peaked barns. She had lived here for the first two years of her life, she thought, and took another long breath. Then, with Lars close behind her, she walked up the wooden steps to the front door and knocked on it.

Pandemonium reigned inside: shrieks of laughter, a child crying, a babble of voices speaking Norwegian at top speed. She knocked again, louder. A man's voice shouted something indistinguishable, then Kristine heard heavy footsteps clump toward the door. She wiped her damp palms down the sides of her shorts and tried to dredge up a smile.

The door swung open. The man was wearing a woolen waistcoat over a white shirt. He was in his seventies, with a grizzled beard, a shock of white hair, and a pair of the bluest eyes Kristine had ever seen. My eyes, she thought in stupefaction, and knew this must be Jakob Kleiven, her grandfather. Forgetting all the speeches she had so painstakingly rehearsed in Norwegian, she said in a brittle voice, "I'm Kristine. From Canada."

When he opened the door he had been laughing. Kristine watched the laughter die away; as it did so, the face became more and more her father's face, older but with the same uncompromising bone structure. He'll never let me in, she thought sickly. He's my father all over again. I've come here for nothing.

He also appeared to have been struck dumb. Wondering if he spoke no English, she stammered, "*Gustav Kleiven... d-datter.*"

In very good English Jakob Kleiven said sternly, "Have you come in anger?"

"No! Of course not." Suddenly it was quite clear what she in turn should ask, for there was no prevaricating with those piercing blue eyes. "Are *you* angry with *me*?" she said.

"No, child, no... you have come all the way from Canada to see me?"

"I've been travelling for two years. My father doesn't know I'm here."

His face darkened. "Ah... Gustav. I wrote to him—two, three letters all those years ago. But never any answer."

She remembered the envelope with the red-and-blue border. "I think he might have torn them up," she said gently.

He nodded slowly, as though she was only confirming something he already knew. "But you are not Gustav," he said. "You are his daughter, come from Canada to see me." A wide smile split his beard. "*Velkommen, Kristine, velkommen.*"

He gathered her into a rough hug. His shirt smelled of pipe tobacco and starch, and there was a glitter of tears in his eyes. Then he held her away from him. "You are so beautiful," he said gruffly. "I see Gustav in you—

your chin and your eyes. And Nina, too. Ach, Gustav—
for a while I thought he had broken my heart, my oldest
son, so dear to me.''

''Will you tell me why he left?'' Kristine asked.

Astonished, Jakob Kleiven said, ''You don't know?''

''He would never tell me. Nor would my mother.''

''Yes, I'll tell you. But not now. Later...'' And he
kissed her on both cheeks, ceremonially. ''Kristine, you
have made me very happy today.''

''I was so afraid you wouldn't want to see me.''

He was ushering her in the door. ''Come in, come in,
we are having a little party as you can hear...and your
friend here?'' He beamed at Lars, pulling him in the
door as well.

Hastily Kristine introduced him. Jakob gave Lars a
stately bow, then said to Kristine, ''You will meet more
family today than you bargained for—it is Margrethe's
birthday so we are all here. Come along and meet
everyone.''

The room into which he led them was full of people.
Jakob explained who she was in rapid Norwegian, and
out of all the faces surrounding her, faces smiling and
exclaiming, Kristine fastened with deep relief on a familiar one. ''Hello, Harald,'' she said.

''I wondered when you'd get here,'' Harald drawled,
and grinned lazily at Lars. ''Glad to see you caught up
with her.''

''It wasn't easy,'' Lars remarked.

''Kristine, you know Harald?'' Jakob exclaimed,
scowling mightily at his nephew. ''How is that?''

''We met in Oslo,'' Kristine explained hurriedly. ''I
made him promise not to tell you I was in Norway—I
was really afraid you wouldn't want to see me, Bestefar.''

''He most certainly kept his promise,'' Jakob said,
tugging at his beard. Then his smile broke through.
''Now I tell you the names of everyone, Kristine.''

Names and faces were a blur to her; what was clear was that she was welcome. More than welcome. She was hugged and kissed and exclaimed over in English and Norwegian, Lars interpreting when language broke down. A drink was thrust into her hand by a tall young man called Iver. A child of five or six wanted to know if she had ever seen a polar bear. Harald lamented that Gianetta was in Genoa on assignment so couldn't be with him.

Her head whirling, Kristine took a big gulp of her drink, sputtered at its bite, and heard Lars murmur in her ear, "Aquavit—be careful, it's dynamite."

Then Margrethe, whose birthday it was, came up to her. She was carrying a baby of perhaps six months. "This is Sonja," she said shyly, in very careful English. "Will you like to say hello to her?"

Kristine put her drink down on the nearest table and took the baby in her arms. The deep blue Kleiven eyes stared at her unwinkingly, even as the child's weight inexorably carried her back in time to the birth of Carl, eldest of her four brothers. Then Sonja smiled, a fat baby smile full of complicity.

It was impossible not to smile back. As Sonja grabbed a tendril of Kristine's hair and pulled on it, gurgling placidly to herself, Kristine felt with a frisson along her spine that someone was watching her.

She looked up. It was Lars, standing only a few feet away from her, his face inscrutable as he gazed at her holding the blue-eyed child in her arms. Long ago she had vowed she didn't want children. But what if this were Lars's child? What then?

Suddenly it was all too much for her—the meeting with her grandfather, the roomful of relatives, the baby at her breast, the man silently watching her. Filled with a tumult of conflicting emotions, Kristine to her horror felt her eyes flood with tears, tears that spilled over her lashes and streamed down her cheeks. Helplessly clutching the child, she wished the floor would open up and swallow her.

Then Lars was at her side. Swiftly he transferred Sonja to her mother's arms, produced a rapid explanation for the circle of concerned faces, and led her out of the room and through the front door. The sunlight was blinding, the roses a blur. She let him lead her down the steps and across the grass to the wooden fence around the pasture.

A cow with enviably long lashes and a gaze as placid as Sonja's was peacefully chewing the cud. Kristine rested her hand on Lars's wrist and said the first thing that came into her head. "Did the baby remind you of Elisabet?"

He looked down at her fingers. "Yes," he said, "there was that." With one finger he stroked the blue veins on the back of her hand, a simple gesture that reminded her of the nights she had spent in his arms, nights of pure happiness. Then he met her eyes. "But there was more than that. It was quite clear to me in that crowded room that eventually I'd like to have more children. And that I want you to be the mother of those children."

Kristine jerked her hand free, the words coming without conscious thought. "No, Lars—not me."

He said inflexibly, "Deny that you thought of that possibility when you were holding Sonja."

"That doesn't mean I have to do it!"

"I said eventually, Kris. Not this year or next. But some time."

"You're like a glacier," she accused. "Grinding away bit by bit, quite unstoppable."

"In bed with you I'm not like a glacier," Lars retorted, and kissed her parted lips.

The cow butted his ribs with her nose, and Kristine, who had responded with fire rather than ice, seethed, "They're probably all watching us through the window."

"They might as well get used to me—because I'm not going to go away."

"*I'm* going back into the house. I need a good dose of that aquavit."

His eyes full of mockery, Lars said, "Too much of it impairs the sex life, *elskling*."

The words came from somewhere deep inside Kristine. "You know what, Lars? At some level you still scare the hell out of me." Then she turned on her heel and ran for the house.

The party had picked up momentum in her absence. Trays of open-faced sandwiches had appeared, along with beer and wine; sticking to her word, Kristine downed the last of her aquavit, and made a concentrated effort to sort out some of her relatives. Margrethe was Harald's sister. Their mother Mari was Kristine's aunt, the one who through the years had kept in touch with Kristine's mother. Knut and Edvard, one portly and one very thin, were her uncles. Iver, who had given her the aquavit, was Margrethe's husband. Not one of them mentioned her tears. Kristine began to enjoy herself, and as she relaxed her small stock of Norwegian came back to her.

A cake bright with candles was carried in by Karoline, Jakob's stout, white-haired sister. Knut, the portly one, went to the piano, Edvard produced a fiddle, and they all started to sing. Before long, as the sun disappeared behind the mountain peaks, they were dancing, folk dances that wove intricate patterns on the old wood floor.

It was past midnight when everyone went to bed. Harald had also brought a tent. Kristine went sedately to hers and Lars to his, and within five minutes she was asleep.

The next day the family started to filter away. Harald drove off in his sports car, the uncles went back to their respective farms, and Margrethe's family left for

Balestrand. Midmorning a haying crew arrived from the village to fork the sweet-scented grass over long fences to dry. Jakob gave the orders while Kristine carried beer and sandwiches to the crew, among whom was Lars, stripped to the waist and plainly enjoying himself.

She sat down beside him to eat lunch, Great-Aunt Karoline's straw hat perched on her head. The heat of the sun, the lazy drone of insects, the rustle of hay cast a spell that was irresistibly sensual. There were flakes of grass and dirt caught in the tangled hair on Lars's chest, and he smelled of sweat and hay. He said softly, reaching past her for another sandwich, "I'd like to make love to you here, in the grass."

As though he had touched her, her body filled with an ache of desire and her limbs grew languid. "It wouldn't take you long to persuade me."

He looked around. "We only have to get rid of eight other people."

She loved that elusive gleam of laughter in his face; yesterday's conversation about children receded in her mind. "Have some more beer instead," she said limpidly.

In the afternoon, while the crew labored under the sun, Jakob invited her to sit with him on the rocking chairs in the shade of the front porch. He went straight to the point in a way she was realizing was characteristic of him. "It is a brief story but not a happy one, why Gustav left Fjaerland," he said ponderously. "But you wish to hear it?"

"Yes. I'm hoping it will help me understand why my mother and father are the way they are."

"Well, then...Gustav never liked farming, even though he was the oldest of my sons and the land would be his. The village was too small for him, he said, there was not enough excitement. So he went away to Oslo, boasting of the wonderful job he would get. But within a year he was back, and would say nothing of what he had done there."

Jakob began tamping tobacco into his pipe with his thumb. "He met Nina, who was pretty as a picture, and they got married and moved in here with me. Soon you came along and I was happy, for he had settled down, I thought." He lit a match, frowning. "While he was away we had formed a cooperative in the village for fishing and farming, and Gustav took over as treasurer—that too made me happy. But two years later we discovered he had been cheating it of money all along. Stealing from the villagers. From his own people and his kin."

The match blew out in the breeze. "My son," Jakob said, his voice heavy with an old anger, "nothing but a common thief."

Kristine sat very still, waiting for the rest. "We had a terrible fight, he and I," Jakob went on, clearing his throat. "I wanted him to work on my farm to pay back the money. He laughed in my face and two days later was gone, he and Nina and you, my little granddaughter. He left a letter on the kitchen table saying he was going to Canada and would never come back to Fjaerland."

No wonder her father had hated the orchards and farms where he had worked. And no wonder her mother had always been so sad, for she had been torn from her village under a cloud of disgrace. Kristine said in a low voice, "I don't believe he ever stole again. But he's never been happy again either."

"When you go back I want you to take a message from me. The farm is still here, tell him, and I would welcome him home."

She blinked rapidly. "I'll tell him, yes. But I have no idea how he'll respond. He never allowed us children to speak Norwegian—and the boys all have English names."

"Perhaps the message is enough. That we forget the anger after so many years."

Jakob went on to give her more details, then Kristine told him about her life as a surrogate mother for four small boys. The work crew came for their money, Lars headed for the bathtub, and Kristine went inside to help Karoline with dinner. She had done what she had come to Norway to do, she thought, slicing tomatoes that were still warm from the garden. Before long she must go home and give her father Jakob's message.

Home to Canada. Leaving Lars behind.

Three days passed. Lars was gone all day, joining the haying crew on other farms along the fjord. Kristine, appreciating his tact in leaving her alone with Karoline and Jakob, missed him horribly, and spent the evenings in an agony of sexual frustration that she sincerely hoped was invisible to the rest of them. On the fourth day it rained. Lars perforce stayed home.

He and Jakob tucked themselves in a corner in the living room and played chess, wreathed in Jakob's tobacco smoke. And Kristine didn't know which was worse—having Lars gone all day or having him underfoot in the house.

The rain had stopped by early evening, and Karoline had been shooed out of the kitchen. Up to his elbows in suds in the old-fashioned kitchen sink as he washed the dinner dishes, Lars said, "Let's go for a walk to the foot of the glacier, Kris."

She carefully put down the pottery bowl she had been drying. She liked it when Lars used the diminutive of her name. But she honestly didn't care if she never saw another glacier in her life. How could she feel like snapping Lars's head off and tearing the clothes from his body at one and the same time?

"It'll be dark soon," she answered unhelpfully. And the grass is soaking wet so we can't make love in the field without my grandfather knowing what we've been up to, she added silently.

"One night at my brother's cottage would make both of us feel better," Lars said, as though he had read her mind.

"You flatter yourself," she snapped, and grabbed a handful of cutlery from the rack. Three of the knives slipped through the cloth and clattered to the floor. She bent to pick them up, adding wretchedly, "I'm not normally bitchy. What's wrong with me?"

Lars pulled her to her feet, getting suds on the sleeves of her sweater, and kissed her with a combination of frustration and desire that caused her to drop the knives and the cloth and to clutch him with unashamed fervor. Then he released her. "Maybe the sight of all that ice will cool us down," he grated and turned back to the sink.

She picked up the knives and dropped them into the water again. "I wouldn't bet on it."

He lifted Karoline's bread pan. "Why don't we take off for a couple of days, Kristine? I'd like to show you Dalsnibba and Geiranger...then we could come back here."

"Yes," she said.

His grin was boyish. "I like a woman who knows her own mind."

"This has nothing to do with my mind, Lars," Kristine said primly, and put the cutlery away in the drawer.

Twenty minutes later they took the path that led through the trees to Supphellebreen, Lars setting a fast pace that Kristine was more than happy to emulate. If she tired herself out she might get a decent night's sleep, something she hadn't had since she had left the cottage.

Getting dependent on Lars, Kristine? a mocking voice whispered in her ear. That's not travelling light.

Go away, she adjured it. This is about sex. Nothing else. Just sex.

As she bounded incautiously up the slope, a cedar tree dumped a day's worth of raindrops on the back of her shirt. And then she came out into the open and saw in front of her the high crest of the glacier at the top of the mountain. At the base of the cliff was another great mound of ice, dirty ice pockmarked with fallen rocks, connected to the glacier by waterfalls that tumbled down rifts in the rock. A river swirled around the cliff, the water pale as milk in the twilight.

With a crack like thunder a piece of ice broke free of the glacier and crashed down the mountainside.

"Some of that ice is five thousand years old," Lars said. "They've had as many as fifteen avalanches here in twenty minutes."

Kristine gazed at his profile, which merged into the rock behind him. Somehow he had made peace with his past in a way she, so far, had not. He had gone to the deserts of Sudan and the jungles of Malaysia to do so; whereas she had come to Norway...

Over the ceaseless splash of the river she heard a new sound, a strange, high-pitched sound like that of an animal in distress. "What's that?" she said sharply.

"Jakob told me there's a herd of horses near the foot of the glacier—let's take a look."

Lars began pushing his way through the tangle of tall shrubs that lay between them and the river. When they reached the edge, Kristine saw a wide strip of grass lapped by the pallid waters of the river. Milling around on the grass were the dark shapes of several horses, the bells around their necks clanging, their wild neighs splitting the dusk. She also saw, with a surge of pure rage, the reason for their distress.

Two men were standing on the riverbank, men in black pants and leather jackets. They were firing rocks at the horses, and even as she watched a rock struck a foal in the ribs. It squealed with pain and one of the men laughed raucously, bending to pick up another stone and wading out into the river to get closer to the horses.

"We can cross down river and get behind them," Lars rapped. "Come on."

They raced along the bank, then waded the river; although the water was, not surprisingly, extremely cold, it did nothing to cool Kristine's anger. They ended up behind the two men, both of whom were now in the water. The mare was trying to coax the foal into the river on the far side of the grass; a rock struck her flank and she whinnied with fury.

Kristine had spent a lot of time outdoors with her brothers, partly in an effort to get them away from the oppressive atmosphere of the house, partly to escape from it herself. She could climb trees with the agility of a monkey and was a mean hand with a catapult. She now picked up a round stone, hefted it in her palm, and fired it with deadly accuracy at the nearer of the two men. It hit him on the back of his neck. He yelped with pain, swung around to see where the rock had come from, and lost his footing. Grabbing at empty air in a futile attempt to keep his balance, he sat down hard in the river.

When the other man turned to see what had happened, her second rock struck him in the belly. He doubled over, slipped, and banged his elbow against a boulder. His bellow of outrage gave her immense satisfaction.

Lars said, "You could take your place in a Viking ship any day of the week."

As she looked over at him, the fire of battle still blazing in her eyes, he reached out for her and kissed her mouth.

"I like you, Kristine Kleiven," he said, his voice midway between passion and laughter. "And now it's my turn. That little foal could have broken its leg."

With vicious strength he threw a stone that hit the first man on the shoulder as he was struggling to his feet. Lars's next shot glanced off the second man's knee. He and Kristine were invisible through the screen of bushes on the riverbank, and she was not surprised when the two men started scrambling with ungainly haste for the shore. Lars said softly, "They're not hikers...let's at least get their license number and report them. The parking lot's this way."

She followed him through the bushes, ducking low, branches scratching her bare legs. Then they were running across the grass past some trees. From the corner of her eye Kristine caught the shine of metal and veered to the right, straining to see through the shadows as darkness blended trees and grass and rocks into the flatness of night. Motorbikes, she thought. That's what I saw.

Before her brain could process that there were three bikes, not two, she ran straight into the third man, the breath knocked from her lungs. As he grabbed at her, she heard the other two men shout something behind her, and twisted to free herself. But her face was jammed into a shirt that smelled of stale sweat, and the man had a grasp like a gorilla.

Her Swiss army knife was on the bureau in her bedroom at the farm.

Then everything happened very fast. A dark shape loomed behind her assailant, there was a flurry of blows, in the course of which she was unceremoniously dropped, and Lars gasped in mingled aggression and amusement, "Run for it, Kristine—back the way we came."

The other two men were crashing through the bushes toward them. She grabbed the ignition key from the nearest bike, memorized the number on the second one, and as the owner of the dirty shirt thudded to the ground under the impact of Lars's fist she dashed through a gap in the trees, Lars close on her heels.

They ran hard, keeping to the shelter of the undergrowth as much as they could. When they reached the river, Lars waded in, taking Kristine's hand because the current was deep. He pulled her up the opposite bank and into the black-shadowed alders, put his arms around her and kissed her again.

Her chest heaving, Kristine wrapped her arms around his neck, kissed him back very explicitly, and knew she would have made love with him here on the ground in the cold night air. Lars muttered, "We shouldn't hang around. I wouldn't put it past them to come after us... I got two of the plate numbers, what about you?"

"One set of numbers and one key," she said, triumphantly dangling it in front of his nose.

He gave a sputter of laughter. "You've got a thing about keys, haven't you? I'm glad you're on my side."

"Thank you for rescuing me," Kristine added. "He needed a bath—ugh."

Lars flexed his muscles. "About time I proved my manhood."

"Oh," she said, "there are other ways you could do that."

"Tomorrow night we'll stay in Geiranger," he said forcibly, taking her hand and leading her through the bushes. "Four nights of celibacy have been more than enough."

For her as well. Her wet shorts were clinging to her legs and water was slurping in the toes of her sneakers; shivering, Kristine wondered how she would ever manage without him on the other side of the Atlantic.

CHAPTER TEN

THE final descent to Geiranger was a series of hairpin
turns down the side of a mountain, with a spectacular
view of the vertical cliffs and azure waters of the fjord.
As Lars drove slowly down the hill, he glanced at
Kristine's hands, which were clenched in her lap. "Not
much longer," he said.

"I'm okay, really...did you ski again after the avalanche, Lars?"

"I made myself go skiing two days after the funeral—
or else I might never have gone." He smiled crookedly.
"Bestemor was outraged that I could do anything so
frivolous when I should have been home mourning."

He took another sharp turn, his eyes on the road.
"Since then I've skied in Switzerland and Austria and
even managed to enjoy it...see that building way down
the fjord, by the water's edge? That's where our cabin
is. It'll be quieter there than in the center of town."

She had to go back to Canada soon, Kristine thought
with preternatural clarity. But she wasn't leaving today.
She still had tonight with Lars. Tonight and tomorrow
and tomorrow night before they went back to Fjaerland.
That was future enough.

In the double bed in the cabin by the water's edge she
and Lars came together that night in an explosion of
feeling that overwhelmed Kristine with its primitive force.
That she was also frightened by the strength of her own
emotions she did her best to hide both from Lars and
from herself. She slept in Lars's arms, she woke to his
lovemaking, and in a daze of physical satiation she ate

a late breakfast in the little restaurant overlooking the glassy waters of the fjord.

A spider had spun a web between two shrubs just outside the window; dewdrops clung to it, and the delicate threads trembled lightly as the spider made some repairs. The web's design was exquisite. Yet as Kristine gazed at it an unwary moth was suddenly trapped in its sticky mucus. So it was also lethal, that beautiful web. Like the Viking ships, she thought, and heard Lars say in an amused voice, "Kristine, for the third time, would you like more coffee?"

With a little start she saw that he was holding the china coffeepot poised over her cup, his fingers curled around the handle. Fingers that had touched her body in ways that a month ago would have been beyond her imagining. She felt hot color creep up her neck and mumbled, "Yes, please."

Some of the coffee sloshed into the saucer. Lars muttered something under his breath and said abruptly, "Let's go to Dalsnibba this morning. The sky's clear so it would be a good day to be on top of a mountain."

"As long as I don't have to climb it," she said darkly.

He chuckled. "You can drive right to the top. It's not like Prekestolen."

Nor was it. A dirt road wound its way up the side of the mountain to the peak, where a mile above sea level there was a large parking lot. As Kristine got out of the car, she hastily reached for her jacket and pulled it on over her sweater, because the wind had a winter's bite to it. Then Lars led the way out onto the rocky slopes of the mountaintop.

Kristine looked around her in awe. Not a tree or a shrub was in sight—only a tumble of gray rock, split by frost, worn by weather. In cracks and crevices tiny plants huddled from the wind, clinging to the scraps of soil. And all around her, at the same level as she, were the peaks of the surrounding mountains, smoothed by distance, their slopes coated with a dazzle of snow and ice.

Lars held her hand while she peered over the edge of Dalsnibba to see the way they had come, the tidy green fields of the valley a dizzying distance below, the road a thin gray thread that doubled back on itself time and again. Geiranger Fjord looked impossibly tiny, a teal blue puddle under the blue sky. They then walked away from most of the other tourists to a lake whose clear cold water slapped in noisy waves against thick chunks of translucent ice.

A few high clouds had appeared in the sky, dappling the landscape with shadow. Kristine sat down on a rounded boulder and took a deep breath of the achingly pure air. "This is a wonderful place," she said. "I'm so glad we came, Lars."

He had been gazing around him at the sweep of the mountains, snow, and sky, and almost unwillingly brought his eyes back to her face. The sun slanting across his features, he said, "I've often imagined that a marriage could be like this—space and immensity, height, depth and breadth..."

Kristine's muscles tensed, her nails digging into the rock, for he had taken her by surprise and she knew him well enough to sense that this was no idle conversation. I don't want to talk about the future, she thought, and said noncommittally, "I suppose that's one way of looking at marriage."

"Room to breathe and room to grow."

In the sunlight his eyes were even more blue, demanding a response of her. In a spurt of anger, kicking at the shards of stone beneath her feet, she said, "Marriage can also be like this—rocky ground where nothing grows because there's no soil, no nourishment."

"The most beautiful Arctic flowers bloom here in the spring."

Her nostrils flared. "The mountaintop's covered with snow ten months of the year."

He took two steps closer, resting one foot on the boulder that she was sitting on, leaning his arms on his knee. "Let's cut out the fancy language, Kris. You know what I'm leading up to—I want you to marry me."

With immense effort she did not back away from him. Shaking her head, she said in a stifled voice, "I can't do that, Lars—I don't want to."

He said quietly, "There's a word we've never used between us, isn't there? A word I've longed to say when you've been lying beside me in the night, or when I've woken to find you curled into my body in the morning...love, Kristine. You see, I love you." Briefly a smile lit his face. "Maybe I have ever since you did your best to cripple me in the park in Oslo, I don't know. I do know I love you now and that I'll still love you ten and twenty and thirty years from now. And that I want to live with you at my side night and day, and to share with you the joy of children, and to be together for the rest of our lives."

A lump as cold as ice had lodged itself in Kristine's breast and she was having difficulty breathing. "Don't do this, Lars—please don't spoil everything," she pleaded, warding him off with a gesture that spoke volumes.

He leaned a little farther forward, his eyes pinioning her to the rock. "It won't spoil anything, I swear it won't."

She covered her face with her hands, unable to bear the intensity of his gaze. "I don't even want to hear that word love!"

"Don't pretend you didn't know I was falling in love with you."

Kristine dropped her hands, staring at him with something like hatred. "You said we'd have fun together, that's all. Share fun and laughter and adventure. We've done that—and now you're ruining it.''

"So you thought this was just a game?" he said incredulously. "Something to while away the summer, a month-long affair and then we'd go our separate ways?"

"I never asked you to fall in love with me," she said defiantly. "In fact, I did everything I could to discourage you. I was certainly honest with you from the start about how I feel about marriage."

With a careful lack of emphasis Lars said, "And nothing's changed for you in the last three weeks, Kristine? Our stay at the cottage—that didn't show you that love between a man and a woman can be full of joy and intimacy?"

Kristine bit her lip, remembering all too clearly some of the intimacy they had shared, in bed and out. Clutching at straws, she said, "I can't possibly marry you—I'd go crazy living at Asgard."

"My grandmother's going to leave Asgard to my brother—that's the other thing she and I sorted out after you left Oslo. I've never wanted Asgard as he does. That's why I applied for the UN job."

Furious with him for so neatly undermining her position, wishing she was anywhere else but marooned on a mountain peak, Kristine cried, "I don't *want* to get married, Lars! How many times do I have to tell you that?"

He straightened, took her by the wrist and drew her to her feet. Then he said with an air of calm logic that infuriated her, "We wouldn't have to get married right away—we could live together for a while if that would make you feel better."

"You're missing the point—I'm not into commitment of any kind," she responded stormily. "Yes, we've had an affair, and it's been wonderful. I've——"

He cut through her words. "You said something to me the very first time we made love, Kristine . . . you said you wanted me to be myself with you. Do you remember that?"

"Yes," she said. Anna's fears had tamed Lars, diminishing him from the man he was meant to be. She, Kristine, had never wanted to do that.

"I've been myself with you—you've freed me from the trap of the past. But if you truly want me to be myself you must accept that I love you, because that's part of me. I love you, and I want to marry you."

Feeling besieged on every side, she said helplessly, "I know I said that, and I meant it—but just because you love me doesn't mean that I automatically love you back. Life doesn't work that way—it isn't that tidy and predictable."

His mouth tightened at her words. She hated herself for saying them; yet they had had to be said. "Please," she added, "can't we go now? And forget this ever happened?"

He dropped her wrist, taking a step back. "You might be able to forget it," he said grimly, "I can't. Don't you see what's going on here, Kristine? Two days after the avalanche I went skiing, because I knew if I didn't I might never put on a pair of skis again. You're still hiding your skis in the closet. Yes, your parents had a lousy marriage, and your mother robbed you of your childhood into the bargain—you've got every right to be angry with them. But if you cut yourself off from marriage and the chance to have your own child you're not allowing yourself to heal. The past is running the show . . . don't you see that?"

"And what if I decide I hate skiing?" she retorted. "So much so that I'm going to give it up altogether?"

"You don't hate it," he said with total conviction. "Don't forget that you and I lived together for nearly two weeks. I know how much passion you're capable of, I've heard you laugh until you cry, I've watched you swinging on the hammock smiling up at the sky. You're as different from your mother as—as I am from your father."

"Stop it, Lars."

"Deny that we were a partnership when we routed those men who were stoning the horses. Deny that you thought of bearing my child when you held Margrethe's baby at your grandfather's . . . dammit, Kris, don't shut yourself up in a cage of your own making!"

Each word he uttered battered at Kristine's composure, tearing away the certainties that had upheld her for so many years. And if she allowed those certainties to vanish, what was left? The risk of throwing her lot in with a man she had known just over a month?

He's also the man who saved your life, and who's brought you incredible happiness, a betraying inner voice told her.

"Love doesn't last," she said desperately, as much to herself as to Lars.

A faint smile removed some of the intolerable tension from Lars's face. "I won't be able to prove that it does until we're dandling our great-grandchildren on our no doubt arthritic knees."

Kristine bent and picked up a rock, firing it into the lake, where it thunked against a block of ice. "And what if I say I don't love you?" she said. "What then?" She raised her eyes and looked him full in the face.

A muscle twitched in his cheek. "I won't believe you."

But she had seen doubt and fear chase themselves across his face, and pushed her advantage. "You must— because it's true. And that's the real answer to your proposal of marriage, Lars. I won't marry you because I don't love you. So there's nothing more to say."

He thrust his hands in the pockets of his Windbreaker, deep lines indenting his face. "You're not telling the truth," he said. "You're hiding behind——"

"Lars, I don't love you!" She took a step back from him, her heel inadvertently crushing a tiny Arctic anemone, exhaustion settling on her shoulders like a deadweight. "I want to go back to Fjaerland."

White about the mouth, he said, "Maybe you don't love me now...but if we keep on seeing each other you——"

She had to end this. "No," she said.

A muscle jumped in his cheek. "If I take you back to Fjaerland today, I won't be stopping—I'll go straight to Oslo."

"That would be best," Kristine said.

"And I won't be back. Ever."

"There's no point in you coming back. Because I can't give you what you want."

Behind him the waves sloshed against the ice. He said bitterly, "I thought I knew you, Kris, knew you through and through. All this talk about love—you're hiding behind those words, using them so you won't have to face how afraid you are of commitment and intimacy...I never thought you were a coward."

Stung, she said, "I'm a realist—there's a big difference."

"At least Anna admitted her fears, was honest about them," he blazed. "You're not even that."

In hot denial Kristine spat, "I'm not being dishonest if——"

"Yes, you are! And let me tell you something else—I don't need to be with a woman whose life is run by fear. I went through that once, and I never will again. I thought I could be myself with you—but I was wrong. Dead wrong." Biting off the words, his eyes like chips of ice, he added, "I've had enough of this. More than enough. We'll check out of the hotel and then I'll drive you back to Fjaerland. Because in one respect you're most certainly right—you can't give me what I want."

Turning on his heel, he started back to the parking lot, and if he stumbled, he who was normally so nimble of foot, Kristine was in no state to notice. The vast, majestic panorama of mountains and sky seemed to mock her, for Lars was wrong—marriage offered no similar long view but rather a cage, confinement as tight as a narrow black dress. Confinement she was right to fear.

Lars took the steep, winding track down the mountain as fast as was safe; the drop-off was on Kristine's side of the car, and made her feel physically ill. When they reached the hotel, it was with a huge reluctance that she entered the bedroom where she and Lars had made love only a few hours ago. Made love... that word again, she thought miserably, stowing her garments in her backpack any which way.

She said stiffly, "I could get a bus to Fjaerland. I'm taking you out of your way."

He looked at her across the bed as though she were a stranger. "I'll take you," he said, and threw his razor into his case.

Kristine never forgot that drive from Geiranger to her grandfather's. Although it was not very far, for which she was everlastingly grateful, it seemed like a thousand miles. She felt paralyzed inside, as if she had been anesthetized, and for that, too, she was grateful. Small talk was out of the question, and she and Lars had said everything else there was to say; so they sat side by side in the car in a charged silence that screamed with tension.

Each turn in the road, each tunnel and incline, brought her nearer the farm that she was calling home, the place she could hardly wait to reach; yet when the Jaguar turned up Jakob Kleiven's driveway she was surprised that they had arrived so soon. Lars spoke for the first

time since they had left Dalsnibba. "I'll get my stuff
and say goodbye to Jakob and Karoline."

He was out of the car door and taking the front steps
two at a time before Kristine could think of any reply.
As she heaved her backpack from the back seat and followed him into the house, her grandfather came out of
the kitchen wreathed in smiles. "Karoline has made fish
cakes, lots for all of us—we weren't expecting you until
tomorrow."

Kristine said baldly, "Lars is going back to Oslo."

"Not before supper...he'll never taste fish cakes the
equal of these in Oslo," Jakob boomed. "Anyway,
what's his hurry? Nils is haying the day after tomorrow
and could do with help."

Incapable of telling either the truth or a lie, Kristine
said nothing. Above her head she could hear the floor-
boards creak as Lars moved around his room packing;
then he came downstairs and into the living room. He
held out his hand to Jakob, speaking so rapidly in
Norwegian that Kristine could not follow what he said.
Jakob asked a question, gesturing in the general direction of the kitchen, and Lars shook his head, adding
another spate of Norwegian. Although it was clear Jakob
was still prepared to argue, the two men shook hands.
Then Lars turned to Kristine.

In her jeans and a sweatshirt she was braced against
the chesterfield. He said coldly, "I can always be reached
via my grandmother at Asgard. Safe travelling, Kristine—because that's what you've chosen, isn't it?"

"Goodbye," she muttered, pressing the backs of her
knees into the plush fabric. She didn't love Lars. She
didn't. Why then did she feel as though her heart was
turning to ice within her chest?

He left the room, his footsteps echoing on the wooden
steps outside. As though pulled by a force greater than
herself, she walked to the window and watched him throw

his case in the back seat and get in the car. Without giving the farmhouse another glance he drove down the narrow lane to the road. Within seconds he was out of sight behind the trees.

Jakob said with a casualness that grated on Kristine's nerves, "A pity he had to leave so soon—I'll miss our chess games. He was a worthy opponent. Ah, well, business comes first, I suppose. And it's all the more fish cakes for us, eh, Kristine?"

The thought of fish cakes turned her stomach. Yet it would appear Lars had fabricated a reason for his leaving that had satisfied Jakob, and she had no intention of telling the real reason for his departure. "Excuse me for a minute, Besse," she said, and fled up the stairs.

She had the second floor to herself. She crept along the hall to Lars's room and looked in. The bed was made, the dresser bare of personal effects; there was no sign that for five nights he had slept here. He was gone. Gone without a trace.

Kristine went to the bathroom, locked the door, and leaned on the basin, looking at herself in the wavery old mirror. She looked the same as usual. Yet her stomach was churning and her hands as cold as if she had dipped them in the lake on Dalsnibba. Lars was gone. He would not chase after her ever again, as he had in Mandal and Stavanger. This time he was gone from her life and he would not be back.

I did the right thing, she thought dully. I can't marry him if I don't love him.

The old cow bell, Karoline's signal for mealtimes, clanked in the downstairs hall. Hastily Kristine splashed cold water on her face and ran downstairs.

While Jakob, to her great relief, asked no questions about Lars's precipitate departure, he did have a tendency to drop his name into the conversation in a way that scraped on Kristine's nerves. She begged out of her grandfather's offer to start teaching her to play chess that evening on the excuse that she was tired, and went to bed early, only to lie awake for most of the night. The next morning when she went downstairs some of the haying crew were in the kitchen, three handsome, blond young men who left her totally unmoved. Lars should have been with them, leaning against the counter, joining in their jokes and horseplay.

Her throat hurt. Maybe she was getting a cold, she thought, taking an orange out of the refrigerator and making a gallant attempt to respond to the repartee of the three young men. Then one of them mentioned that Arne, the tractor driver, was sick. She said eagerly, "I grew up on a farm, I can drive a tractor," and realized how badly she needed something concrete to do.

So Kristine's days fell into a pattern. Up early in the morning to spend the day in the fields, home for supper, and a chess lesson in the evening with Jakob, who would all too often describe at great length details of Lars's strategies. Physical tiredness would then drive her to bed, where sexual longing and emotional exhaustion kept her awake.

After four days of this regime it rained. Kristine tried to sleep in and failed, helped Karoline make blackberry jam, and then escaped to the barn to clean out the stalls. The barn was peaceful and smelled of hay; the swallows darted among the eaves. If Lars were here, she would want to make love with him in the hayloft...

"Kristine?"

Kristine jumped, dropped the pitchfork, and said foolishly, "Oh, Margrethe, it's you." Margrethe, Harald's sister. Not, of course, Lars.

"I scared you, I am sorry." Margrethe came closer. "But you look so tired. You are sick?"

Heartsick, thought Kristine, her eyes skidding away from the sympathy in Margrethe's face. "I've been out haying the last few days," she said, and saw from Margrethe's delicate withdrawal that the other woman would ask no further personal questions.

"Jakob works you too hard," Margrethe said with a little click of her tongue. "Will we go to the house and make some tea?"

To her utter dismay Kristine heard herself blurt in a voice raw with feeling, "It's nothing to do with haying. Lars asked me to marry him and I said no and now he's gone."

Wishing the words unsaid, she picked at the rough wood of the stall with her thumbnail, avoiding Margrethe's eyes. Margrethe said calmly, "You have changed your mind?"

"No! I don't love him, so how can I marry him?"

"You cannot—you did the right thing, Kristine. Although I can see it was difficult. He seemed a fine man."

You're no help at all, thought Kristine. If I did the right thing, why do I feel so unhappy?

"Mind you," Margrethe added, "I think it is as important to like your partner as to love him. But then I have been married only five years. I am not—what is the word?—an expert."

"Love doesn't last," Kristine burst out. "My parents don't love each other any more."

Margrethe said with more force than Kristine had yet seen in her, "I love Iver and he loves me. I do not know how that will be in five years, ten years, twenty years. I hope and pray we will still love each other—but I do not know. That is how life is, Kristine."

The monolith at the sculpture park fell into Kristine's mind, that mass of seething humanity, interconnected in love and in suffering. She said hesitantly, "So you think I'm looking for guarantees?"

"I do not suggest you marry anyone before you know him well. Do you like Lars? Do you trust him? Is he a good man, a kind man? I love my little Sonja . . . I must know that Iver will be a good father to my child. All these are questions to ask before you trust your life with another person." She gave a self-deprecating smile. "I sound like the pastor on Sunday morning, I am so sorry."

Kristine's head was whirling. "What *is* love?" she said.

"Ah...I don't know." Margrethe frowned in thought. "Perhaps it is like the many petals of a rose—together they make a flower that is beautiful."

Kristine's throat tightened. "Thank you, Margrethe," she said, adding with a smile that was almost normal, "Let's make that cup of tea."

After tea the rain had stopped, and Kristine volunteered to look after Sonja while Margrethe and Iver went for a walk. She lay down on the carpet beside the baby, singing it some of the nonsense songs she used to sing to her brothers, and because Margrethe had been honest with her she forced herself to a matching honesty such as she had been avoiding ever since Dalsnibba. As Sonja's pudgy fingers tugged at her hair, she knew in her inner heart that she did not want to close off the doorway to having her own child.

Her fear of pregnancy had nothing to do with babies. Pregnancy implied commitment. Pregnancy implied a husband, a man who would be a good father for the child. A man like Lars?

Jakob sat down in the chair near her, lit his pipe, and said heavily, "In the kitchen Margrethe said I must be gentle with you because you are unhappy about Lars— she thought I knew the real reason why he left. Were you afraid to tell me the truth?"

It was quite clear her grandfather's feelings were hurt. Kristine said in distress, "I'm sorry! I'm so confused, Bestefar. Lars asked me to marry him and I said no."

"Ach...so that was it. Urgent business, Lars told me—pah! Well, if you don't want to marry him, that's that, isn't it? You must put him behind you."

"Yes," Kristine said in a hollow voice.

Jakob shot her a crafty glance that she missed because she was playing with Sonja's toes. "He is too old for you anyway."

"He's not! He's only thirty-one."

"But from a very different background, a wealthy man from one of the old Oslo estates. You are Canadian more than you are Norwegian, and your home is there. These things matter, Kristine. Youth may not think they do, but they do."

"Our backgrounds were never a problem," she said stubbornly. "Anyway, he's not going to live at Asgard."

"And a widower, besides. All these barriers...your decision was wise."

"Besse, we'd worked through all that," Kristine said in exasperation.

With rare delicacy Jakob said, "I'm an old man now, but I have lived—so all was not well in the bedroom?"

She flushed bright pink, buried her face in Sonja's chubby belly, and mumbled in huge understatement, "That was okay."

To her infinite relief Karoline came in the room with a biscuit for Sonja, and the subject of Lars was dropped. The reprieve, however, was only temporary, for that evening as she and her grandfather played chess it seemed to Kristine's overwrought sensibilities as though every second word was Lars. Lars would have deployed his bishop like this. It was a good thing Lars had fixed the drive belt on the tractor. Lars would have enjoyed the fish they had for supper. Lars, Lars, Lars...

Her mind on anything but the game, she made a very silly mistake. "A good thing Lars isn't here to see that,"

Jakob said complacently, removing her castle from the board.

"Would you please stop talking about him?" Kristine flared.

"Why?" Jakob said callously. "He isn't dead. All you did was turn him down—he'll recover."

A detailed image of Lars marrying Sigrid flashed across her mind, filling her with an unpleasant mixture of pain, jealousy, and fury. "It's me I'm worrying about, not him," she snapped, not very accurately.

"Pay attention to your pawn there," Jakob said mildly. "If you're the one who turned him down, I don't see why you're so upset."

Neither did Kristine. Although upset was an altogether inadequate word for the state of dull misery in which she had been trapped since Lars had left. Her grandfather added with irritating certainty, "You're probably homesick. Two years is a long time to be away. Will you travel more before you go back to Canada, Kristine?"

She had no appetite for further travel, and, while it was logical that she go home, she didn't want to do that either. "I don't know what I want," Kristine admitted. Then, her shoulders slumping, she added with genuine desperation, "I turned Lars down because I don't love him. I'm sure I was right to do so...tell me what love is, Bestefar."

Jakob sat back in his chair, tamping the tobacco in his pipe. "I'm not sure that your father ever loved your mother," he said deliberately.

"Never?"

"She was very pretty and she thought the sun rose and set on him, and the job he had in Oslo hadn't worked out. So he married her. But love...no."

So love, in her father's case, had not died. It had never been born. "Did you love your wife?" Kristine asked.

"Always. We fought sometimes—oh, how we fought— she was stormy-tempered, from an island far in the north, and sometimes for her my farm was like a box, too small and too tidy. Every year she would go home to Hasvik for a visit, every year I would be afraid that she might not return, and every year she came back to me. Yes, I loved her." He held a match to his pipe, his eyes trained on the small yellow flame. "Love isn't always easy, Kristine. But after thirty years of marriage I still knew when she walked into the room. Knew it in my heart."

"Thank you for telling me about her," Kristine said huskily.

He shot her a keen glance. "I watched you and Lars when you were here together. And I was reminded of me and my Sonja when we were young and in love."

Briefly Kristine closed her eyes. If Lars were to walk in the room right now, wouldn't she know it in her heart? Of course she would.

"Harald is coming for the weekend," Jakob said slyly. "He'll be going back to Oslo on Sunday."

And if she went back to Oslo, what would she do? Walk up the front steps of Asgard between those two hideous griffins, and announce to Lars that love was like the many petals of a rose?

Harald arrived on Saturday, marched up through the field to the vegetable garden where Kristine was weeding, and said coldly, "What the devil's wrong with you, sending Lars away like that?"

Kristine had not had an easy week. She hauled out a thistle, shaking the earth from its roots, and said, "Mind your own business, Harald."

"I thought you had more guts than that!"

"I have a perfect right not to marry Lars," she said haughtily. "Or anyone else for that matter."

"Not when it's as clear as the nose on your face that you're crazy about him."

"So is that your definition of love? Being crazy about someone doesn't seem much of a basis for a lifelong relationship."

"Okay, Okay, it was a poor word to use. To me it looked as though you loved each other from the start."

"It's not nearly that clear to me," Kristine said shortly. "As I keep saying to the point of boredom, I don't even know what love's all about."

"That's obvious." But the anger had died from Harald's face, and as he sat back on his heels, absently brushing flecks of earth from his pants, his face was unusually thoughtful. "Do you want to know what I think love is, Kristine?" he said soberly. "It's our only way of dissolving our separateness. Take me and Gianetta. Two people from different cultures and speaking different languages. Yet when we're together— and I don't mean just when we're in bed, although that's part of it—sometimes we're able to become one." He paused, searching for words. "To complete each other and do away with the barriers we spend so much of our lives creating and defending. Open to each other." He shrugged, adding with his normal charming smile, "I can't explain it. It's got something to do with basic body chemistry, too—and you and Lars certainly had that."

"Yes," Kristine said with painful truth, "we did have that."

"Why don't you give it a second try? You could go back to Oslo with me tomorrow," Harald said lazily, flicking an insect away from her face. "In the meantime, do you want me to bring you a beer?"

"Please," she said, and watched him lope down the hill.

The beauty of a many petaled rose. The human need for closeness and union, the trust that allowed for vulnerability. The stormy-tempered wife who chose to live far from the freedom of her island home because she loved her husband. Maybe, Kristine thought, knitting her brows, there are as many definitions of love as there are people, and I have to discover and trust in my own.

The sun lay warm on her bare arms, the scent of freshly turned earth filled her nostrils, and she missed Lars so acutely that she almost cried out with the pain of it. If she went back to Oslo with Harald tomorrow, she could see Lars tomorrow night—hear his voice, feel his hands on her body, watch laughter glint in his gray blue eyes. Know that she made him happy. Be happy herself. And begin the long journey of trusting in that happiness, a journey she would take not alone, but with him at her side.

The back door opened and Harald appeared carrying two bottles of beer. Kristine bent to her weeding, and wished with every ounce of her strength that it was Lars who was walking up the slope.

CHAPTER ELEVEN

ON SUNDAY evening at eight-thirty Harald drew up in front of the stately stone mansion called Asgard. "I'll wait here," he said, a mocking gleam in his eye. "This is your scene, babe."

Kristine said with great dignity, "That's outmoded slang, Harald." Then, in sudden panic, "What if he's not here?"

"Leave a message. With anybody but the grandmother."

She took a deep breath, got out of the car, and shook out the folds of her blue dress. Then, holding herself very upright, she climbed the steps, ignoring the griffins, and rang the doorbell.

Her heart beating like a trip-hammer, she heard the lock scrape and watched the door swing open. As the butler inclined his head, she asked for Lars in her best Norwegian.

"He is not at home, madam."

Kristine bit her lip, wondering if the extent of her disappointment was any measure of this elusive emotion called love. "May I please speak to Fru Bronstad?" she asked.

He ushered her in the door and led her down a long hall to a parlor she had not seen before, a room minimally less gloomy than the dining room, with, Kristine saw with a quiver of pain, a bouquet of old-fashioned roses on a mahogany armoire. Marta Bronstad was seated in a straight-backed wing chair, reading. She looked up when Kristine came in, and said with neither overt surprise nor particular warmth, "Miss Kleiven...do sit down."

Kristine chose the nearest chair, which was oak, carved like the prow of a Viking ship and about as comfortable. She said with a calmness she was far from feeling, "I came to see Lars."

"He isn't here."

So this was to be like a chess match, thought Kristine, a series of moves by players who were opponents. "Please could you tell me when he'd be home?"

"I have no idea. He's left Norway, Miss Kleiven."

Whatever Kristine might have expected, it had not been that. Her poise deserting her, she croaked, "Left *Norway*?"

Marta Bronstad inclined her head, then sat in a majestic silence waiting for Kristine's next move. Fighting down an utter desolation that Lars should have gone from Asgard, Kristine felt the beginnings of anger, healthy and alive, lick along her veins. Deliberately she went on the attack. "Lars asked me to marry him," she said, "but I turned him down."

The old lady said coldly, "So why are you here looking for him?"

It was the most difficult question she could have asked. "That's a personal matter between the two of us," Kristine said, and knew it for a weak reply.

Marta Bronstad folded her hands tidily in her lap. "Unfortunately, as I have already said, he is not here."

"When did he leave?"

"Early in the week."

"When will he be back?"

"He promised to come home for his birthday in October," Marta said with a smile that was a mere movement of her thin lips.

October. She would have to go back to Canada long
before that. "And will you tell me where he is?" Kristine
asked.

"Why should I, Miss Kleiven?"

Her eyes blazing, Kristine abandoned discretion in a
glorious sweep of rage. "If your grandson loved me with
all his heart and wanted to marry me—you note I say
'if,' Fru Bronstad—would you want him to be happy
with me? Or would you stand in the way of his happiness because I'm a footloose and penniless Canadian
of whom, clearly, you disapprove?"

"You have a talent for going to the crux of the
matter," the old woman said with grudging respect, the
diamonds flashing on her fingers. "Now I have a
question—why did you turn him down?"

Too angry to be anything but honest Kristine said,
"Because I was afraid. Afraid of love and afraid of
commitment. Afraid my marriage would turn out like
my parents' marriage."

"I have no patience with cowards," Marta snapped.
"Life can be cruel—you take what joy you can and you
don't waste your time searching for guarantees."

Inadvertently she had been given another definition
of love, Kristine thought, and remembered that Lars had
linked tragedy with his grandmother's life. She said
carefully, "So there are no guarantees?"

"None." Staring at a point beyond Kristine's shoulder,
the old woman said, "My husband, whom I loved, was
killed in the war. My only son, Lars's father, died in an
accident along with his wife when Lars was six. No, there
are no guarantees."

Instinctively Kristine offered no easy sympathy. "You
love Lars," she said.

"I love both my grandsons. For although love can
destroy us with its pain it will not release us from its

claims...that is perhaps what you fear, and you are right to do so."

It was a strange moment for Kristine to feel a kind of peace settle on her for the first time since Lars had left Fjaerland. "Thank you for being so open with me," she said.

Marta leaned forward, impaling Kristine with her fierce old eyes. "Do *you* love Lars?"

Kristine's gaze was drawn back to the roses, whose dusky petals were clustered around the flowers' golden hearts. "Yes, I love Lars," she said, and in a flood of incredible joy knew her words for the truth. She was not certain what she meant by those words; but in the sureness of the emotion that filled her heart was the germ of her own definition of love.

The blue eyes that she raised to Marta's face were brilliant with the wonder of her discovery. The old lady leaned back in her chair, adjusting the folds of her dark skirt. "Lars is in New York, being interviewed for the UN job—I will give you the name of his hotel."

Kristine let out her breath in a long sigh; she had not expected such generosity. "Thank you," she said again, and thought how odd it was that she should find out she loved Lars in the gloomy parlor of a house she disliked, with a woman who was a redoubtable foe.

"Will you go there?" Marta asked.

"Yes. I have an open return ticket...I'll go as soon as I can get a reservation."

Marta said with a touch of malice, "Maybe he'll no longer want to marry you."

Buried deep down, Kristine was afraid of the same thing. She said dulcetly, "If that's true, then I was right to decline his offer of marriage, was I not?"

To her utter amazement, Marta Bronstad laughed, a laugh creaky from disuse, but nevertheless a laugh. She rang the silver bell on the table beside her and said, "You'll join me in a glass of sherry, Kristine?"

Knowing she had won a major victory, Kristine for the third time said, "Thank you," and hoped her jaw hadn't dropped at this quite unexpected use of her first name. The parlor did not look nearly as gloomy as it had when she entered, and on the armoire the roses glowed with pagan color.

Giddy with jet lag, Kristine stood on the edge of a New York pavement and studied the entrance of the hotel where Lars was staying. It was within sight of the tall green trees of Central Park and the expensive bustle of Fifth Avenue, and she was quite sure its brochures would describe it as exclusive.

While it was time for a midmorning coffee break in New York, Kristine's inner clock was telling her it was 4:00 a.m. The overnight transatlantic flight had allowed her very little sleep and had left her with a dull headache, so that she neither felt nor looked her best. Her pack, containing her entire wardrobe, her tent, and her sleeping bag, was strapped to her back; she was wearing jeans and her best shirt.

The commissionaire standing on the plush red carpet outside the hotel was dressed in a smart olive green uniform, while some of the guests walking in and out of the brass-edged doors could have graced the covers of *Vogue*. Kristine straightened her spine in a way Fru Bronstad would have approved, and approached the door. She smiled at the commissionaire and said, "Good morning."

He touched his peaked cap and held the door open for her as if she were a visiting duchess. Much encouraged, Kristine crossed the foyer, receiving a quick impression of glorious hothouse flowers and twinkling chandeliers, and said to the young man at the reception desk, "I believe Lars Bronstad is a guest in your hotel. I wonder if you could page him for me, please?"

The young man was not as gracious as the commissionaire. He gave Kristine's attire a swift, critical assessment before saying with automatic courtesy, "One moment, madam."

He touched several keys on his computer and waited for the screen to display, then said coolly, "Mr. Bronstad checked out earlier this morning."

"Checked out—you mean he's *gone*?"

"Yes, madam."

"Do you know where?" she gasped.

The young man's voice hardened imperceptibly. "No, madam."

"He didn't leave a forwarding address?"

"No, madam."

Nor would you give it to me even if he had, Kristine thought. Striving for composure, she said with a touch of sarcasm, "Thank you for your help," and headed for the brass-edged doors. The commissionaire saluted her, and she walked away from the hotel exactly as though she had a destination in mind.

She kept walking until she came to a fast-food chain, entered and ordered coffee and a doughnut, then unstrapped her backpack and sat down in one of the booths. The coffee was excellent and the doughnut fresh, but try as she might she could not focus on either of these simple pleasures.

She was alone in one of the world's largest cities. She did not know one soul among the several million souls surrounding her. She had very little money. And she had missed Lars by a matter of an hour or so.

Maybe he's gone back to Norway. Maybe he's gone to Mexico or Guatemala or any of a dozen places that his new job might take him. Maybe he's already forgotten you.

A fragment of doughnut caught in her throat. Coughing, Kristine buried her face in her paper serviette and wondered what on earth she was going to do.

She had an emergency fund of four hundred dollars that she had never touched in her two years of travelling. It would get her home to Ontario. Even if her father didn't want to hear Jakob's message she should deliver it to him.

She didn't want to go home to Ontario. Not yet. She wanted to be with Lars.

She could wait four or five hours to allow for the time zones, and phone Marta Bronstad on the off chance that Lars might have spoken to her with his whereabouts. If that didn't work, she could phone the UN and try and track Lars that way—which was probably the modern equivalent of looking for a needle in a haystack.

What she couldn't do was hang around in New York for more than a couple of days. She couldn't afford to.

She whiled away the time with a second cup of coffee, a visit to the Metropolitan Museum, and a light lunch. Then she found a public telephone and began the complicated procedure of phoning Asgard, whose number Marta Bronstad had written down for her. After a series of clicks and beeps, the phone began ringing. The butler answered, Kristine asked for Fru Bronstad, and in a few moments the old lady's tart voice came over the line. Speaking as distinctly as she could, Kristine said, "This is Kristine Kleiven. I'm in New York. Lars checked out of his hotel this morning."

With the nearest thing to warmth in her voice Marta Bronstad said, "I'm glad you phoned. Lars spoke to me last night after you left—he's gone to stay at the country home of one of the directors for three days, his name is Charles Franklin, and his home is in a little place called Lambourne, in the Catskills. The nearest town is Tranton. Do you think you can find that?"

Kristine was busily taking notes in her address book. "Yes," she said, "I'm sure I can."

"I chose not to tell him you were flying to New York...I hope I did the right thing?"

Marta Bronstad was actually asking her opinion. Kristine said solemnly, "Absolutely."

"Do you have money for a proper hotel? New York can be a very dangerous place for a woman on her own."

"If I managed in Istanbul, I'm sure I can manage in New York," Kristine said dryly.

There was a small silence. Then Fru Bronstad replied with equal dryness, "Most certainly you will make a more interesting addition to the family than Sigrid. Good luck, my dear." And she hung up.

Kristine was left gaping into the receiver. Hurriedly she replaced it and began searching for the number of the bus station. After a frustrating exchange with a computer, she discovered she could get a bus to Lambourne leaving in an hour and a half. She spent more money on a cab to the bus station, found the right booth and bought her ticket, and then went upstairs to wait.

The bus station seethed with eddying crowds of young men whose vocabulary seemed entirely composed of four-letter words and whose anger was a palpable and frightening force. Kristine kept her pack firmly at her side and was glad Marta Bronstad couldn't see her now.

Eventually the bus pulled out of the station. Although it was a two-hour trip, Kristine was too keyed up to sleep; she gazed out of the window as the concrete of the city was replaced by fields and trees and small towns, and wondered whether Lars would be pleased to see her.

Quite clearly, having travelled all the way from Oslo in Norway to Lambourne in New York State, she was not simply dropping in to see an old friend. Rather, she would be intruding on a private country home, on a gathering to which she had not been invited. A gathering, moreover, associated with Lars's new job. If he no longer loved her, she could be an acute embarrassment to him.

There was a very strong likelihood that he didn't love her any more. After all, what had he said to her in those last dreadful moments on the peak of Dalsnibba? "I don't need to be with a woman whose life is run by fear... You can't give me what I want."

Kristine was so tired that her head seemed to be floating somewhere above her body. Closing her eyes, she watched as the head grew arms and wagged an admonishing finger at her. Grow up, Kristine, its voice said crossly. You saw the strength of Lars's feelings for you. He hasn't changed his mind in little more than a week. He left you—and the country—because he couldn't stand being with you when you'd done such a fine job of convincing him you didn't love him. Get real!

She opened her eyes and the head disappeared. Her legs were twitching with tiredness and her eyes felt scratchy from lack of sleep. She was insane to be chasing Lars across the width of an ocean, travelling burdened down with doubts and fears, her destination in another person's hands.

It could not by any stretch of the imagination be called travelling light.

The finger wagged right in front of her nose this time. But you've joined the human race, it said. You've taken the risk of falling in love. Remember the monolith? You've just become part of it.

She remembered something else: the incredible surge of joy when she had acknowledged to herself that yes, she did love Lars. Hugging the memory of that joy to her, trying not to think about Dalsnibba, she leaned back against the headrest.

Someone was shaking her arm. "The driver says this is your stop," the elderly lady in the next seat was explaining. "You wouldn't want to miss it."

Mumbling her thanks, Kristine staggered up the aisle, waited while the driver got her backpack from the baggage compartment, and watched the bus drive away in a cloud of ill-smelling exhaust.

She was standing outside a gas station that fortunately was still open, for while she had been asleep dusk had fallen. Inside she got directions to Charles Franklin's house in Lambourne, and bought a chocolate bar and a bottle of pop—all that the gas station offered in the way of sustenance. Then she hitched her backpack in place and set off down the road.

The village was charming, yellow light spilling from square-paned windows in salt-box houses, gardens smelling sweetly of honeysuckle and nicotiana. As she tramped along, the houses grew farther apart, set among oak and elm trees amid gently rolling hills loud with crickets. Her frayed nerves relaxed a little.

She passed a crossroads and began counting the houses on the left, the third of which belonged to Charles Franklin. It had a trimmed privet hedge and an elaborately carved gate, and was larger than the other houses. It was also well lit and had a car parked in front of the double garage. So someone was home.

Her heart racing in her chest as though she had just climbed Prekestolen, Kristine started up the cobblestone driveway. Two black Labrador retrievers came bounding to meet her, barking loudly. She let them sniff her hands, then approached the front door, where pink roses were clustered on a trellis. Love is many petaled like a rose, she thought numbly, and pressed the bell.

After an agonizingly long wait a woman's voice called, "Coming!" The outside light was turned on, the door opened, and the entire doorway was filled with a very large woman clad in a voluminous apron. She said comfortably, "Can I help you?"

She exuded kindness, smelled faintly of newly baked bread, and was presumably the housekeeper. "I believe Mr. Franklin has a guest called Lars Bronstad," Kristine said awkwardly. "From Norway. I wonder if I could speak to him for a minute, please?"

"Well, you could if he was home, dear. But the four of them went out for the evening."

"Four of them?" Kristine repeated blankly.

"That's right. Mr. and Mrs. Franklin, and Mr. Bronstad, and Mr. Franklin's sister Heidi. They probably won't be back until midnight—it was a party at a neighbor's."

Heidi . . . Kristine's imagination supplied her with an image of a willowy brunette, cultivated, charming, and rich. "I—I'll come back in the morning, then," she stammered, already backing away from the door.

"Leave me your name, dear, and I'll tell him you were here. Or you could wait inside with Jack and me. We're watching the quiz shows and you'd be more than welcome."

Kristine took another step back and nearly tripped over one of the dogs, who was sniffing her sneakers with a connoisseur's thoroughness. "Oh, I couldn't do that. Thank you anyway," she said with a false smile. "I'll come back tomorrow."

Perhaps.

"Let Jack drive you back to the village, then. It's dark and you shouldn't be out alone."

"Truly I'll be fine," Kristine prattled. "Thank you so much for your help, you've been very kind. Goodbye."

She hurried down the driveway and turned right through the gate. She had noticed a coppice of trees

alongside a brook near the crossroads; she'd sleep there
and in the morning she'd get the bus back to New York.

Lars was at a party with another woman.

Tears of exhaustion and misery stung Kristine's eyes.
That he had every right to be at a party with anyone he
chose because she, Kristine, had sent him away, was im-
material. As jealousy sank its ugly claws into her, she
walked faster, irrationally terrified that he and the
beautiful Heidi—because she would, of course, be
beautiful—might come home early and discover her.

She could not bear to see him with another woman.

There were no houses in the immediate vicinity of the
trees, which were surrounded by hayfields; the brook
chuckled to itself in the darkness. Wanting only to be
out of sight of the road, Kristine clambered over the
ditch and wove her way in among the shelter of the trees.
Only then did she ease her pack to the ground and take
out her flashlight.

She was too tired to set up her tent, and by the look
of the stars spangling the sky she didn't have to worry
about rain. After pumping up her lightweight mattress,
she spread her sleeping bag on top of it, slid into it fully
dressed, and pulled it up to her chin.

Over her head the canopy of leaves rustled together
secretively; from upstream the shrill peeping of frogs
pierced the thick blackness of the night. Lars didn't love
her any more, she thought with utter clarity. No matter
what Margrethe and Jakob and Harald had told her,
love was as changeable as the tides, as fickle as the wind.
Roses didn't bloom forever; the petals shriveled and died.

Lonelier than she had ever been in all her twenty-three
years, Kristine felt tears seep down her cheeks and soak
into her sleeping bag. Then, as suddenly as if she had
been hit on the head, she fell into a stunned sleep.

*   *   *

The bear came closer, its small dark eyes only inches away, freezing her into immobility. Its lips were drawn back from twin rows of yellow white teeth. Its black nose came closer, snuffling at her throat...

With a shriek of fear, Kristine sat upright, pushing at the black head that had buried itself in her throat, animal breath rank in her face.

The Labrador retriever sank back on its haunches, its tongue lolling from its jaws, its coat merging with the blackness of the night. From down the slope a man's voice shouted through the trees, "Kristine! Is that you?"

She heard the scrape of a shoe against rock. Dry leaves rattled underfoot as the beam of a flashlight lanced through the branches. Pulling her sleeping bag against her chest, Kristine huddled into its down folds, not sure whether the bear had been real and she was dreaming the dog, or whether reality was indeed the Franklins' black dog and the approach of Lars.

Then a man accompanied by a second dog stumbled into the little clearing where she had arranged her sleeping bag, and the beam of light struck her full in the face. Blinded, panic-stricken, she gasped, "Go away!"

"Kristine—thank God I've found you."

Lars fell to his knees beside her, dropping the flashlight into the grass as he reached out for her. She struck him away. "I didn't ask you to come looking for me—I should never have come," she cried incoherently. "Go back to the Franklins and forget you ever saw me!"

The flashlight, although lying in the grass, supplied enough light for her to see Lars sit back on his heels, staring at her as though she had gone out of her mind. "If you didn't want to see me, what in God's name are you doing in the Catskills when I left you in Fjaerland?"

"I thought I loved you so I came after you to tell you and then I found out you've already started going out with someone else," she said, the words tumbling over one another. "So I was right all along—love doesn't last, I knew it didn't."

Lars said with deadly quiet, "Will you kindly explain to me what you mean by you thought you loved me? Either you do or you don't. It's not something you turn on and off like the kitchen tap."

"You're darn right it isn't! So how come you've done exactly that, Lars Bronstad?"

"I haven't!" he roared.

The first black dog butted against Lars's chest, whimpering uneasily and nearly overbalancing him; the second had stretched out across the sleeping bag and was snoring asthmatically. Kristine said pettishly, "There's no need to yell."

"If I have to yell to get your attention, then I'll yell," Lars retorted. "I loved you yesterday, Kristine Kleiven, I love you today, and I'll love you tomorrow. In fact, it would appear to be my fate to love you until the day I die. So how dare you accuse me of turning you off like the kitchen tap?"

"You went to a party last night with someone called Heidi," Kristine announced. "And don't bother denying it."

"I went to a party with Heidi tonight," he corrected her. "It is now eleven forty-five exactly. I came home early because I didn't have the stomach for cocktail small talk, and was told by Mrs. Bentley that a young woman with a backpack, blond hair, and eyes blue as the sky— Mrs. Bentley is a true romantic—had been asking for me and had then left without saying where she was going. You're the only woman I know who fits that description, so I've been searching for you ever since."

"And where's Heidi?" Kristine snapped.

"Still at the party, for all I care."

"You really don't care?"

"I really don't care! Heidi's an attractive and pleasant woman and if I never saw her again I wouldn't lose a minute's sleep over her." Lars's voice roughened. "Whereas if you were to vanish again right now, I'd—oh, hell, Kris, I've missed you the last week as though you're my life's blood."

"But you told me I couldn't give you what you wanted," she said in a small voice.

"I know you can," he said forcefully.

As the black dog leaned against Lars's shoulder and closed its eyes in bliss, another piece of Kristine's definition of love fell into place—a piece called trust. Because she instantly believed Lars. He hadn't stopped loving her; of course he hadn't.

Thoroughly ashamed of herself, she said, "I left Oslo—well, I guess it was just last night, although it feels like a week ago. And then I missed you at the hotel by only a couple of hours, and by the time I got here I was so tired I could hardly stand up. When the housekeeper told me you were at a party with another woman, it was horrible, I felt just awful. But I should never have doubted you."

"How did you know where I was?" Lars said in a strange voice.

"Your grandmother." Kristine gave him a small smile. "She thinks I'm more interesting than Sigrid."

"That's one way of putting it." Lars pushed the dog away. "So you came from Fjaerland to Oslo to New York to Lambourne just to find me?" Kristine nodded, wishing she knew what he was thinking. "Why, Kristine?" he asked. "Why did you do that?"

"I was so unhappy after you left," she muttered, picking at the hem of the sleeping bag. "I can't really explain, Lars . . . I don't think I understood what love is all about; I was too afraid of it to admit that I'd fallen in love with you, so I——"

"You *have*?" he interrupted.

"Of course, that's what I'm trying to tell you...when you look at me like that, I can't even think straight," she added, her voice wavering shamefully.

"Come here," Lars said. "Explanations can wait."

He put his arms around her and kissed her with a combination of hunger, happiness and humility that touched Kristine to the core of her being; and once again she felt that surge of incredible happiness that she loved Lars and was loved by him.

Her foot was falling asleep where the dog was lying on it, and the other dog had thrust its nose between them, whining and flailing its tail from side to side. Before Lars could speak, Kristine said, "I love you, Lars," and heard the words hang softly in the cool night air. They were the right words, she thought. The only words.

His face changed. He said huskily, "I never thought I'd hear you say that to me. I love you too, *elskling*." Then, shoving the dog's head aside, he kissed her again.

"I'm so sorry I sent you away," Kristine said, between kisses that brought her body to life and filled her heart with rapture. "I think I needed to be without you in order to understand what you mean to me. Does that make any sense?"

"Anything that brought you back to me makes sense," he said forcefully. "I love you more than I can say, I'll marry you as soon as——" He stopped suddenly, raising his head. "You will marry me, Kristine?"

"Oh, yes," she answered with a radiant smile.

"Good," he said, stroking her breasts through her shirt and leaving a trail of kisses down her throat. "Right now all I want is to take you to bed, and one dog's far too interested in us to let us make love and the other one is taking up most of the sleeping bag...you do realize I won't be able to get you to a hotel until tomorrow night?"

She could feel the smooth play of his muscles under his shirt, while the clean male scent of his skin inundated her with memories. "When your grandmother told me you wouldn't be home until October, that seemed like forever. But now all of a sudden tomorrow night is forever."

"I think it's called relativity," Lars said, laughter warming his voice in the way she had never forgotten. "Something to do with Einstein."

"I do love you, Lars!" she exclaimed, and tilted her head back to laugh in sheer happiness. "Margrethe explained it best—love, she said, is like the many petals of a rose that together make a flower of great beauty. So I trust you, and I know sometimes we'll fight, and I know too that we complete each other." She traced the line of his mouth with her fingertip. "I want to make love with you, and I'll want to bear our child...so many petals and none of them complete without the rest."

"Neither of us complete without the other," Lars added quietly. "I learned that in the last few days."

"We'll still be travelling light," Kristine said with deep conviction. "Light of heart and side by side."

"The best way to travel." Lars grinned. "I got the job by the way, so we'll also be travelling literally."

"Which will give me lots of chances to learn languages," she said contentedly. "I really want to do that."

A rabbit rustled through the undergrowth on the other side of the stream. The first dog pricked up its ears and crossed Kristine's sleeping bag in one leap. The second sprang to its feet, yelping with excitement, and followed the first through the stream, to be swallowed up in the darkness. Lars said, reaching for the zip on her sleeping bag, "I think we should take full advantage of their absence. Tomorrow night's too long to wait and we don't have to make an appearance at the Franklins' for at least another hour."

"Gather ye rose petals while ye may," Kristine misquoted with a breathless laugh.

When the two dogs came back three-quarters of an hour later, having chased the rabbit with much delight if no success, Lars and Kristine were just starting down the hill. They were walking hand in hand and side by side.

Travelling together.

POSTCARDS FROM EUROPE

HARLEQUIN PRESENTS®

Hi—

I'm in trouble—I'm engaged to Stuart, but I suddenly wish my relationship with Jan Breydel wasn't strictly business. Perhaps it's simply the fairy-tale setting of Bruges. Belgium is such a romantic country!

Love, Geraldine

Travel across Europe in 1994 with Harlequin Presents. Collect a new Postcards From Europe title each month!

Don't miss
THE BRUGES ENGAGEMENT
by Madeleine Ker
Harlequin Presents #1650

Available in May, wherever Harlequin Presents books are sold.

HPPFE5

Relive the romance....
Harlequin is proud to bring you

A new collection of three complete novels every month. By the most requested authors, featuring the most requested themes.

Available in May:

Three handsome, successful, unmarried men are about to get the surprise of their lives.... Well, better late than never!

Three complete novels in one special collection:

DESIRE'S CHILD by Candace Schuler
INTO THE LIGHT by Judith Duncan
A SUMMER KIND OF LOVE by Shannon Waverly

Available at you're retail outlet from

HARLEQUIN®

PRESENTS *Plus*

Meet Alex Hamilton. His reputation as a lady's man convinces Marly to teach Alex a lesson he won't soon forget. But the tables turn when Marly realizes she's become the student—and that she's learning how to love!

And then there's Reid Bannerman. Annys quickly discovers that three weeks at sea with Reid, her *ex*-husband, is a long time to spend together—especially when the quarters are close and the attraction between them still sizzles!

Alex and Reid are just two of the sexy men you'll fall in love with each month in Harlequin Presents Plus.

Watch for
GIVE A MAN A BAD NAME by Roberta Leigh
Harlequin Presents Plus #1647

and

FLAME ON THE HORIZON by Daphne Clair
Harlequin Presents Plus #1648

Harlequin Presents Plus
The best has just gotten better!

Available in May wherever Harlequin books are sold.

This June, Harlequin invites you to a wedding of

Promised Brides

Celebrate the joy and romance of weddings past with PROMISED BRIDES—a collection of original historical short stories, written by three best-selling historical authors:

The Wedding of the Century—MARY JO PUTNEY
Jesse's Wife—KRISTIN JAMES
The Handfast—JULIE TETEL

Three unforgettable heroines, three award-winning authors! PROMISED BRIDES is available in June wherever Harlequin Books are sold.

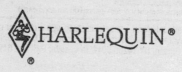

HARLEQUIN®

HARLEQUIN®

Don't miss these Harlequin favorites by some of our most distinguished authors!
And now, you can receive a discount by ordering two or more titles!

HT #25551	THE OTHER WOMAN by Candace Schuler	$2.99	☐
HT #25539	FOOLS RUSH IN by Vicki Lewis Thompson	$2.99	☐
HP #11550	THE GOLDEN GREEK by Sally Wentworth	$2.89	☐
HP #11603	PAST ALL REASON by Kay Thorpe	$2.99	☐
HR #03228	MEANT FOR EACH OTHER by Rebecca Winters	$2.89	☐
HR #03268	THE BAD PENNY by Susan Fox	$2.99	☐
HS #70532	TOUCH THE DAWN by Karen Young	$3.39	☐
HS #70540	FOR THE LOVE OF IVY by Barbara Kaye	$3.39	☐
HI #22177	MINDGAME by Laura Pender	$2.79	☐
HI #22214	TO DIE FOR by M.J. Rodgers	$2.89	☐
HAR #16421	HAPPY NEW YEAR, DARLING by Margaret St. George	$3.29	☐
HAR #16507	THE UNEXPECTED GROOM by Muriel Jensen	$3.50	☐
HH #28774	SPINDRIFT by Miranda Jarrett	$3.99	☐
HH #28782	SWEET SENSATIONS by Julie Tetel	$3.99	☐

Harlequin Promotional Titles

#83259	UNTAMED MAVERICK HEARTS (Short-story collection featuring Heather Graham Pozzessere, Patricia Potter, Joan Johnston)	$4.99	☐

(limited quantities available on certain titles)

	AMOUNT	$
DEDUCT:	**10% DISCOUNT FOR 2+ BOOKS**	$
	POSTAGE & HANDLING	$
	($1.00 for one book, 50¢ for each additional)	
	APPLICABLE TAXES*	$ _____
	TOTAL PAYABLE	$ _____
	(check or money order—please do not send cash)	

To order, complete this form and send it, along with a check or money order for the total above, payable to Harlequin Books, to: **In the U.S.:** 3010 Walden Avenue, P.O. Box 9047, Buffalo, NY 14269-9047; **In Canada:** P.O. Box 613, Fort Erie, Ontario, L2A 5X3.

Name: _____

Address: _____ City: _____

State/Prov.: _____ Zip/Postal Code: _____

*New York residents remit applicable sales taxes.
 Canadian residents remit applicable GST and provincial taxes.

HBACK-AJ